Higher Than The Arrow

Judy Van Der Veer

Higher Than The Arrow

Woodcuts by F. Leslie Matthews

Golden Gate Junior Books

San Carlos • California

c, 1

Copyright © 1969 by Judy Van Der Veer
All rights reserved
Library of Congress catalog card number 68-22393
Lithographed in the United States of America
by Anderson, Ritchie & Simon, Los Angeles
Typography by Continental Graphics

For Marjorie Thayer

Without her this book would not be

Higher Than The Arrow

One

As I was getting ready for school that morning I was glad that straight hair is the style. These days even girls that are lucky enough to have naturally curly hair put on stuff to make it straight. Mama used to take me for permanents but I'd have to put my hair in curlers anyway and it was a bother. All I have to do these mornings is to comb it and brush it and it hangs evenly to just below my ears. Across my forehead I wear a straight bang. It saves a lot of trouble and it looks well-kept, shining and black.

It was cold, so I wore a sweater and skirt. I have lots of clothes—for two reasons. One is that Mama likes to sew and another is that people keep bringing clothes to the Mission. I, who am twelve years

3

old, find it easy to discover pretty things that fit just right.

We live on a canyon side up on the Indian Reservation. Our house is on one of the lower slopes of Higher Than The Arrow, which I think is the best mountain in the world. I'm always looking at that mountain. It is different at different hours of the day and it is different in different seasons. In autumn, when we have dry clear days, its stony peak turns to wonderful colors at sunset. Sometimes it is an amethyst mountain and sometimes it is red and old rose and gold. In winter, and sometimes even in spring, it is white with snow. Before storms the peak is all wrapped up in clouds, and in summer the thunderheads climb above it and turn into fairy castles and strange animals.

But the great thing about Higher Than The Arrow is that it always makes you look up, look high. It makes you feel as if, in a certain way, you could climb high too. It is difficult to explain how that mountain makes me feel. I know that if I had to live where I couldn't see it I'd be homesick.

Every morning we have to hurry to eat breakfast and get ready in time for Mama to drive us down the bumpy dirt road to the highway where we meet the school bus. Early mornings are cold this time of year, just before spring should be coming.

I have two brothers, Jerry and Teofilo. We do not, according to Father Antonio, say Teofilo right. We

4

say it Tee-awful-o, and Father Antonio says it a different way. It means one who loves God. I think that my brother Teofilo loves cars better than anything, though he is an altar boy at church. So is Jerry, who is two years younger than I am. Teofilo is two years older.

Jerry's real name is Jerome, but no one calls him that. For Teofilo there is no nickname, though there should be. *Awful* would be a good one for him because most of the time he is. I am Francesca Clare, but I am called Francie. Our last name is Queri and where that comes from no one knows. It seems to be not very much Spanish or very much Indian. However, there are lots of Queris around as we have dozens of aunts and uncles and cousins. My father, Mathew Queri, is spokesman for our Reservation. Mostly he has to go to a lot of meetings to settle tribal business.

Our car didn't want to start this cold morning, but Mama always parks it where the boys can give it a shove to start it down a slope and usually it is coughing before we roll through our front gate.

There were still patches of snow left in shady places and there was lots of frost. My teacher, Miss Pierce, says that children back east think that it never snows in California, especially in the southern part where we live. They think that there are oranges and green grass and flowers everywhere, all the time.

5

I wish that those children could see our Reservation all covered with snow. Further up on the Arrow the snow stays a long time. Some winters there is too much, and the cattle, poor things, can't find enough to eat; some get so cold and hungry that they die. Most of them come down the mountain to where it should be warmer, but if we have an extra-cold winter it is not warm enough on the lower slopes either.

Years ago there was a good dairyman in the big valley below us and he used to let the Indians pasture their cattle in his valley during the cold months. He said that all the rich valley land used to be ours anyway, and so it was. But he never spoke of giving it back to us.

This morning we got to the bus in time, which was good, because the driver didn't have to wait for us. We had picked up four of the Longtooth children along the way. Their mother and father never bother to drive them to the bus, so they wait for us to come along. These four are younger kids and not special friends of ours.

I don't really have a best friend, though I wish I had.

Mama made sure we had our lunch money and we got on the bus and started another dreary day. I don't much like school.

But one thing about school is good, and that is drawing. I love to draw, especially I love to draw

animals, and I draw better than anyone in our whole school. It is almost always a picture of mine that is chosen for the bulletin board in the hall. Every Monday the best picture made during the past week is put there to stay until the next Monday. Last week I had a charcoal drawing of a deer on the board. Miss Pierce, who is young and pretty, says that I must be an artist when I grow up. She gave me a sketch pad which I keep hidden and take with me when I go out on the mountain alone.

I wish I could make a picture of Miss Pierce. She has soft, light-brown hair and hazel eyes. But I'm not very good yet at drawing people.

I like reading, too. We all like to read in my family, even my brothers. We don't have electricity on the Reservation so we don't have a television. We go to my Aunt Dora's house, down by the paved highway, when we want to see television. The rest of the time we read books we get out of the school library. Mama says we probably never would read if we had television, but kids that have television say that they get tired of it sometimes and like to read once in a while. I don't think that I'd ever get tired of television.

Our school is a grammar school and a junior high both. Kids come to it from three different Indian reservations and from ranches all around. There are white kids and Indian kids and Mexican kids and, from the first grade on up, we have all grown used

7

to one another.

Some people like to say that the teachers pick on the Indian and Mexican children more than the others, but I'm not positive. Miss Pierce picks on me because I am so bad at arithmetic, but I'm halfway good at English and I like music, too. So I am praised for what I'm good at and scolded for being lazy about other things. Miss Pierce watches me because she thinks that when I should be studying I'm either dreaming or drawing pictures behind some big book. And mostly I am.

I am dreaming about something now.

The idea came to me last Sunday when Father Antonio was preaching one of his extra-long sermons. I was thinking how pretty our little Mission church is and, as I was looking at the statues of the Blessed Mother and Saint Joseph, I wished we had a Saint Francis. We certainly should have one of him, out here in the hills where there are so many animals. Of all the saints, he loved animals the most.

Suddenly I thought, well, why can't I try making one?

I went on dreaming about it. I could model a little statue out of clay, and I could ask my Aunt Ophie to put it in fire for me to make it come out hard. Aunt Ophie makes pottery all the time and she'd know how. The more I dreamed, the more excited I became. It seemed like a wonderful thing for me

to do. Of course I'd never made a statue, but I could learn.

Already I have started making sketches of how Saint Francis should look. Perhaps he will have a baby goat in his arms and birds on his shoulders. I'm not sure. If it comes out right I will have Father Antonio bless it and maybe it will be good enough to put in the Mission. I wish I could get it done by Easter. Easter is the most beautiful time of all in our church.

I'm keeping this a secret because I'd like to surprise Mama and everyone else. Of course, if Aunt Ophie is going to help me she'll have to know about it, but she won't tell.

And I had better hurry because, the way things go, it will be Easter before we know it.

Two

THAT DAY there was a new girl in our room. She
didn't come to school on the bus; her mother
brought her to get her entered. I don't know where
she comes from but her father has just gotten a job
working on one of the dairies, the one in the valley
nearest to our Reservation.

Her name is Lucy Olson and she has yellow hair,
cut short and straight, and she has bright blue eyes.
I could tell that she felt scared the first day in a new
school. She only spoke when the teacher spoke to
her and then she didn't talk very loud.

In the cafeteria at lunchtime a white girl in our
class talked to her and sat beside her, but I could
see that she still didn't have much to say. I bet it

would be hard to live in a new place and go to a new school. I have lived in the same place all my life, ever since I was born and my mother brought me home from the hospital. I'm lucky, I guess.

I was planning that, on the way home, if Lucy still looked lonesome, I would sit beside her on the bus and maybe think of things to say to her. But I didn't have to because one of the Swiss girls, whose father also works on the dairy, found a place beside her.

I really was glad not to sit with her because I didn't want to have to talk. I wanted to keep thinking about my statue of Saint Francis. I had tried some sketches behind my geography and I had about decided against the baby goat. I had a brand-new idea, and I liked it.

My idea was exciting because it was something different. Instead of having Saint Francis hold a little tame animal, I wanted him to show a loving feeling for wild animals. I thought that I would like him to be holding a coyote pup. Not a tiny one but a half-grown one, at the thin and gangly age, the age when animals always look pitiful to me. This is the age when perhaps they need help the most. It is when they are beginning to lose their mother's protection, when they must first start to think that perhaps they will have to look after themselves. This must be a very sad time for young animals, when before they have thought that their mothers would always take

care of everything.

I like coyotes, maybe because people shoot, trap and poison them. I never did shiver, the way most small children do, when I heard them at night. They have a hard time, and they are smart and beautiful and I love making sketches of them.

When we were small, Papa used to sing an old Indian song to us. It was in our Indian language and it was a lullaby, though it had an exciting tempo—a sort of "Indianish" beat to it, so that you thought of drums when you heard it. It was about "go to sleep little baby or the coyote will get you." It made me laugh when Mama translated it because I never had thought that a coyote would get me.

In the stories that old people tell about Indians and animals the coyotes are important and greatly admired. It is too bad that everyone seems to have forgotten this these days.

I had a great deal to think about on that bus ride. Of course I realized that I had started dreaming and getting ahead of myself before I'd even made a proper sketch for the statue. But, in my thoughts, I had my statue done, ready to be placed in the Mission church where people could light candles before it.

Next, I thought about how some rich tourist would see it and ask who had made it. Father Antonio would say, "A little girl did it, a girl named Francesca Clare Queri." Then the rich tourist would

13

say, "Oh, you must take me to this child, I must give her lots of money and have her study art."

It came to me that for birds on my statue's shoulder it would be fun not to have humble sparrows or doves, the way you usually see them with Saint Francis, but to have a hawk instead, or maybe even an eagle. A roadrunner might be good, too . . .

I was in such a daze of dreams that I didn't wave good-by to anyone when it was time to get off the bus. I scarcely noticed the new girl and the Swiss children walking toward the dairy. I didn't even say hello to Mama when she met us at the foot of our road. She looked at me sharply and asked, "What is wrong? Did you have trouble from the teacher today?"

"No," I said, coming back to the present. "I was thinking about something. Mama, would you still know where to find our family clay place?"

Mama looked surprised, so I added, "I thought it would be fun to try making a clay pot, the way Aunt Ophie does. Maybe she could show me how and I could sell it to a tourist for money for an Easter dress."

Mama said, "I'm already planning on making you an Easter dress, but that's a good idea about the pot, anyway. Your Aunt Ophie probably still goes to our place. She would show you where it is, I'm sure." Each Indian family always has had its own special place for getting clay. But in our family none

14

of us makes pottery any more except Aunt Ophie.

Teofilo said, "Why don't you find your very own place, Francie? It would be more fun that way."

"Yeah," said Jerry, "we could all go looking this afternoon. I think I saw red earth somewhere."

Mama said, "First you have to fill the woodbox."

My brothers sighed dismally. You'd think that bringing in wood for cooking and warmth was about the worst job in the whole world.

I hurried out of my school clothes and into jeans and tennis shoes. I pulled on an old sweater. By that time the boys had brought in enough wood so Mama was willing to let us go.

Our old dog Jack came with us as we started walking up the canyon. The canyon sort of burrows into our big mountain, climbing as it goes, and you can climb pretty high by following it.

We had had enough rain this winter so that there was water flowing in the canyon creek. It sounded pretty, though it sounded cold, too. The willows and cottonwoods and sycamores were all bare and shivery-looking, but the live oaks were dark green because their foliage never sheds off. Every spring they grow new leaves which push off the old ones. The tiny new leaves are a pinky-lavender color as they unfold.

We passed some cows that didn't look very fat, but once spring is really here the grass will grow thick and tall and the cattle won't have to stay thin

15

and hungry for very long. We saw the three old burros that live up there by themselves and roam around wherever they like. The boy who once owned them is dead.

He used to ride one of the burros to church and would tie him to the graveyard fence. Sometimes, if Father Antonio's sermon was too long, the animal would start to heehaw and we'd all giggle.

This time of year the burros were so shaggy in their winter coats that we couldn't tell how thin they were. We called to them and they looked at us with their buttony eyes and put their long ears straight up. Two of them are gray, the color of mice, and one is brown. We could have ridden them but we hadn't brought any ropes along and, anyway, it was warmer walking.

We left the canyon trail and found a deer trail through the brush. It took us up to a ledge, a little shelf on the mountain from which we could look down on the canyon and the tops of trees. It was a clearing where brush didn't grow and there was grass, still short and not thick. Jerry walked to one end of the ledge where the earth was bare. He said, "See this red ground here. Isn't it clay?"

"I guess so," I answered, staring at the earth that was still moist from the last rain.

"Wish we'd brought something to dig with." Teofilo took up a stick and began to scrape and dig a little.

I picked up a handful of earth. I squeezed it and it did seem to behave like clay. I decided I'd take it home and ask Papa if it really was.

"Oh, boy!" said Teofilo suddenly. "I wish I'd brought a gun!"

There, at the other end of the ledge, at the edge of the brush right by a big boulder, stood a coyote.

"Don't scare him," I whispered.

Right away I knew who he was. He was *my* coyote, the one I wanted for Saint Francis. He was a thin young one and his face was all sharp and triangular. His pointed ears were alert and he was staring at us curiously. He was near enough so I could see that he had a little nick in one ear, as if once some animal had bitten him. His winter coat didn't look thick or warm or healthy enough; even his tail wasn't very bushy.

Our dog Jack didn't see him, he stood so still.

Before I could stop him, Jerry picked up a stone and threw it. Thank goodness he missed, and the coyote melted into the brush.

I was furious at my brothers. "What did you go and do that for? I'd like to hit you with a big old rock."

Teofilo said defensively, "Coyotes are no danged good."

"They kill chickens and dogs and cats," Jerry added.

"So do people," I said. "People do more killing

than anything. I hate people. I hate you!" I turned and hurried down the trail. I was so mad that I didn't even enjoy the bright sunset. It was the color I love the most, too—the raspberry-tasting color. I was so mad that I had tears in my eyes.

I wouldn't speak to my brothers the rest of that day.

Three

THE NEXT day at school I had a chance to talk to the new girl. We were in the girls' room and I was combing my hair in front of the big mirror. She came along and started to fix her hair. We each looked at the other's reflection and smiled.

Lucy said, "Your hair is so black and shining. I wish mine were like that. My hair's awful."

"But it looks great with your blue eyes. How do you like being in a new school?"

"It's kind of funny at first. I guess it will be all right. I just don't like school very much."

"I hate it," I said. "I'd rather be outdoors, out on the mountain. But I really do like Miss Pierce."

"She's nice."

Before we could think of anything more to say, the bell rang. Back in class, I wondered about Lucy. I wondered if she didn't like school for the same reason I didn't, that it made me feel caged in. Lucy might be one who felt as I did. Perhaps Lucy would have been mad, just as I was, when my stupid brother threw the rock at the coyote.

To me, the appearance of that little coyote up on the ledge had been a special message, a sign. It was as if he were showing me that I had the right idea about my statue, that of course Saint Francis should hold a young coyote. And he had looked exactly the way that I had imagined he should.

Now, my trouble was myself. I was still so mad at my brothers that every time I started seeing the coyote in my mind, I'd start seeing Jerry throwing a stone and I'd hear Teofilo wishing for a gun. My anger and my exasperation got in my way so that when I did try the first sketches they didn't turn out right at all. I really had to work before I could produce even one fairly good one.

I made a copy of it and gave it to Miss Pierce to put on the bulletin board in the hall. Even if it didn't quite satisfy me, I knew that it would be better than any picture any other kid could make.

I must have been guilty of what Father Antonio calls the sin of presumption for, the following Monday when we went to school, I glanced at the board to see my coyote—and looked instead at a picture

of a black-and-white cow and a new-born calf. The picture was a water color and the grass was green and the sky blue and there was a blue pond and a white-trunked sycamore. My mouth must have fallen open. Then I heard some kids giggling, so I pretended that I didn't care and hurried on to my homeroom.

I hadn't even looked to see who had signed the picture. I felt odd. Though I hated to admit it, it was a very good water color.

When it came time for art period Miss Pierce made a little speech. "I'm proud to know that there are now two outstanding artists in this class," she began. "We are fortunate to have both Francesca Queri and Lucy Olson. It is from our room each week that a picture is so often chosen. Now, with *two* exceptional artists, we are sure to have an even better record."

So it was Lucy's water color! I could feel everyone staring at me to see how I was taking what Miss Pierce had said. I didn't know which way to look. Finally, I glanced across at Lucy and she smiled at me. It was a timid, friendly smile and I forced myself to smile back. After all, I really did know that the coyote sketch I had made wasn't so very good.

My trouble was that I wasn't very used to having anyone make a picture that was better than mine. Besides, I'd been taken by surprise and that made it seem worse. I tried to tell myself that, since someone

21

had made a better picture, I should be glad it had been Lucy.

I decided that I'd been half on the way to liking Lucy. I'm funny, I guess, but I'm not too quick about choosing to be friends with anyone. I won't make the first move. What if I like someone very much, then come to find out that he or she doesn't like me?

It's queer how many things you think about when you're sitting in school, supposed to be studying history or English or arithmetic. Before I knew it, I was thinking again about Saint Francis and the coyote. I made up my mind that I wasn't going to draw any more pictures for the bulletin board. Instead, I decided I'd keep on making sketches until I got a really good one. Then I'd really know how my statue was going to look when I finished it.

That night at supper Jerry had to tell about what had happened at school. He piped up, "Francie didn't get her picture on the board in the hall this week." I gave him a look that should have seared him.

"What happened, Francie?" Mama asked quietly.

"Nothing. I just didn't feel like making a good picture, and I didn't."

Papa helped himself to more stew, then asked, "Who did win?"

"It isn't *win*, like a contest." I started to explain but Jerry had more to say.

"Some white girl won. A new girl. Her father

works for the dairy. And Francie's mad."

"I'm not either. Except at you for being so stupid."

"Francie's mad about the picture," Teofilo had to put in.

Mama said, "It's nice for a little white girl to win for a change. Francie does so good that it's time someone else had a chance. Isn't that so, Francie?"

Sometimes Mama pleases me enormously. I gave her a look that her warm brown eyes reflected back to me, and she smiled. Mama is kind of fat but she has the prettiest face and the best kind of smile.

Now I felt even more glad that I was planning to make the statue. Mama would be proud of me. I felt more determined than ever to work very hard and make Saint Francis and his coyote perfectly beautiful.

The next day after school I decided to go back up the mountain to the ledge where we'd seen the little coyote. I'd be so pleased if I could see him again. This time I wouldn't have Jerry and Teofilo with me to spoil it all. I wouldn't even let the dog go. I felt a little mean about this because Jack loves to go where we go and I hated to disappoint him. He is a dear old dog and perhaps he hasn't too much time left to have fun in. But I was afraid he might scare the coyote away.

At the last minute I had an idea. I filled a little bag with Jack's dog food, the kind of stuff called kibble that Mama buys at the store. I thought I'd

leave it where the coyote could find it. He had looked as if he could use any kind of food.

When I had climbed up to the ledge I put down the kibble and went to the far end of the clearing. I sat down in the sun, which would soon be gone as night was coming. It felt good and it seemed to me that today was a little warmer than it had been.

I sat very still and stared off across the canyon to the hills beyond. I hoped and prayed that the coyote would come. I kept saying inside me, "Come, little coyote." I sat so still that some wrens came near and I saw a brush rabbit hopping along.

Suddenly, there was the coyote staring at me. I could hardly believe it. I looked and looked and looked, memorizing the sharpness of his face, the sorrow of his thin young body. Now I could see exactly how I would sketch him and I could scarcely wait to have a pencil in my hand. I almost didn't breathe I was so busy looking and memorizing.

Even as I stared he, suddenly self-conscious, vanished. Yet when I started down the trail, I had the feeling that he was watching me from some hidden place. I hoped that he would enjoy the food I'd left him. Papa says that coyotes are so smart the older ones won't touch anything that has human scent. But this one, young and hungry and inexperienced, might not know to be afraid of my scent.

I'd be glad to bring him some food every day, though I didn't want him to grow bold about people.

24

Any wild animal that isn't afraid of people is in terrible danger. Perhaps it was good that Jerry had shown him that humans are dangerous. Perhaps, for his safety, I should be throwing stones at him instead of bringing him food.

But I couldn't do that. I wished he could know that some people are bad, but that I loved him and wouldn't hurt him.

Four

THIS TIME I couldn't go wrong. Every sketch I made of the coyote pleased me. I thought I had made him look young and hungry, and that he also wore a look of dignity, an expression that said he was interested and eager for life. I sketched him in a number of different poses, for my imagination was working well.

I made one of him sitting as a dog sits, his tail curved around his cold little paws. This sketch seemed to me to be the most touching one of all—as if there he was, waiting and hoping for something good to happen.

Though I was still determined not to make any more pictures to go on the school bulletin board, I

could not resist turning this one over to Miss Pierce.
She was pleased, and she surprised me by saying
something that made me know she was on my side
about coyotes. "Coyotes are more valuable than
people think. Without them we'd have too many
rodents."

I agreed. "They don't do all the things they're
blamed for, either," I told her. "Every time people
see a coyote eating a dead calf they say he killed it,
when probably it died anyway. You ought to see
cows when they have calves. One old cow will be
baby-sitter for a whole batch of calves while their
mothers graze, and you ought to see what happens
if even a dog goes near. The whole herd's after him.
A coyote wouldn't have a chance."

Miss Pierce was interested. "Cow baby-sitters! I
never heard of such a thing. Francie, you could tell
me lots of things I don't know."

"Yes, ma'am," I said, suddenly feeling both em-
barrassed and happy.

I supposed that Lucy would be hard at work drawing something for next Monday's bulletin board,
but I felt sure that this time she wouldn't make it.
And she didn't. It was my little coyote that had the
place of honor.

I decided I ought to find out more about Saint
Francis if I were to make a good statue of him, so one
afternoon I set out to see Father Antonio. Except
when he preaches sermons that are too long, I like

him a lot. I was sure he would know all about Saint Francis and would help to make him seem like a real person to me.

We have the prettiest little Mission church and usually I like to go inside to look at the light coming through the colored windows. Today, though, I went right up to Father's house and rang his doorbell.

"Come in," I heard him call, and I did.

He came out of the kitchen to greet me. "Francie! How good of you to come. How you been?"

Father Antonio belongs to a missionary order which sends priests to us all the way from Italy. He is lively and when he gets excited his Italian accent is more pronounced. When he smiles his brown eyes smile first, then the rest of his face, so you know that he really feels a smile and isn't just being polite. Now he smiled at me and said, "What can I do for you, Francie? I know what you can do for me."

He led the way to the kitchen where there was a stack of dirty dishes in the sink. Usually the Indian ladies take turns helping in Father Antonio's house, but apparently none of them had been around lately.

"I've had so many sick calls to make," Father apologized. "This time of year all the old people get down."

I pinned a dish towel around me and went to work. It was fun to wash dishes where water came hot right out of the spigot. In our house we have to heat water on the stove. I said, "I think it's awful that

none of the ladies came to help you."

"Well," said Father Antonio cheerfully, "probably it is good penance for me."

"Penance, Father! Surely *you* don't have to do penance!"

Father Antonio laughed at my shocked face. "Oh, yes. Priests are people too, with all kinds of sins. I could most easily have the sin of pride, or presumption, or one thousand others."

"Then," I said, "I better not wash these dishes. I don't want to spoil your penance."

At that, Father Antonio, who is slightly fat, laughed so hard he jiggled. "I'll dry for my penance." And he found a dish towel.

"You said the sin of pride, Father. Which one is that?"

"Francie! Whattsa matter with you? You been to catechism."

"Yes, but I forgot. Is pride always wrong?"

"Not always. But sometimes. Like a man, he's all stuck-up for having too much money. Now take you. You can be proud of your people and you can be proud to be an artist. But not all stuck-up. Be proud and be humble. Be grateful about your gift."

I brought the conversation around to where I wanted it. "Wasn't Saint Francis rich and proud one time?"

"Saint Francis of Asissi. You know I went to Asissi once?"

"You did?"

"Yes, I did. And there's a mountain there. That saint, he had a mountain when he was a little boy, just like you have that one you call Higher Than The Arrow."

"Like our mountain? Oh, Father!"

"Well, a mountain is a mountain, though they aren't all alike. Mountains make us look up. The people that wrote the Bible, they wrote much about mountains. And Our Lord, He was always going up to the mountain."

"So Saint Francis played on his mountain when he was little? And saw wild animals maybe?"

"Probably. He had beautiful horses to ride. His papa, he was rich."

"Then what happened, Father?"

"Well, he decided he'd give it all up and follow Our Lord. His family, they thought he was crazy. So did his friends. But Saint Francis had found out how to be happy and he wanted to stay happy. So he gave up all his fine clothes and his horses and after that he walked wherever he went."

I thought it was a pity that Saint Francis had given up his horses. They must have missed him. "If he liked animals he should have worried about his horses."

"Maybe he did. But he knew they'd have good care in his rich papa's stables. He liked everything. He liked birds and animals and children and old

31

people because he loved God so much he had to love everything that God made."

"I suppose he'd be good to coyotes, too."

"They didn't have any there. But yes, he'd have liked them too, if he'd known about them."

"Next time you don't get at washing dishes, Father, put them to soak. Then it's easier."

"All right. If I catch the time. Saint Francis, he also made many songs about how beautiful everything was. He walked around trying to help people, trying to follow the ways of Our Lord as much as he could. And later he received the stigmata."

"Stigmata, Father?"

"Francie! You never heard that before? Saint Francis thought so much about Our Lord on the Cross nail marks began to show on his hands and feet."

"Oh. Yes, I heard that somewhere, but not that name. Or I forgot if I did."

I stood holding a soapy, wet dish and thinking that I'd have to put those marks on the hands of my statue.

"Why is it that you ask all about him? Because you have his saint's name?"

"Partly. Father, I'll tell you a secret. I don't want anyone to know about it. But what I want to do, more than anything in the world, is to make a little statue of Saint Francis out of clay. Do you think I can?"

Father Antonio looked at me with delight. "Why, Francie! You betcha your boots! You want to do this that much, and you think about it and—not only that—you pray about it, you can do it."

I laughed at his enthusiasm. I like the way Father Antonio runs all his words together when he grows excited. *Not only* became one quick word with two t's in it.

Then I sobered. "But maybe I can't. I don't want to make a statue that isn't good. It has to be the very best. I'm really not sure that I can. All I know for sure is how very much I want to. What do you *really* think, Father?"

"Like I told you, I think yes. An artist, he must have faith in himself. You must have the faith, Francie, that you, with God's help, can do it. Why not?" It is hard for Father Antonio to talk without using his hands. He very nearly dropped a dish. He waved his towel as he spoke. "I have a little book about that saint which you can take home and read. Then you'll know him better. He was once a soldier, you know, a young officer."

I was in a hurry to see the book so I scraped fast to clean the last of the pots and pans. Finally I could dump out the dish water and rinse the sink. I dried my hands and we went into Father Antonio's study. His desk was a jumble of papers and books and his bookshelves were crowded.

"Here it is," he said after a while, sounding sur-

prised that he had found the book.

I thanked him and hurried away. I felt all happy and sure of myself. Nothing could stop me now. I was going to make a beautiful statue of Saint Francis and the coyote.

Five

I DECIDED that on Saturday I'd go to the coyote's ledge early in the morning and stay there a long time. Maybe I'd see him again. I planned to take something to dig with so that I could get some clay. Then I'd go to Aunt Ophie's.

Saturday morning, when I was ready to leave, Mama nearly wrecked my day. "You'll go nowhere," she said, "until you've cleaned your room. Don't you ever hang anything up?"

"Oh, Mama," I protested, "I'll clean it later."

"Now," said Mama, who can be firm.

So I tidied up my room, which I had to admit was a mess. Then Mama and I got the lamps cleaned, the wicks trimmed, and coal oil poured in.

My brothers had gone with Papa to work on the mountain. Papa's business is making cedar fence posts to sell to ranchers; also he gets oak wood for people's fireplaces. He works harder than any other man on the Reservation.

Finally, Mama let me go. I told her I was going to get clay to take to Aunt Ophie so that she could show me how to make a pot.

Aunt Ophie lives in a little house farther up the canyon and she is usually glad to see me because she lives all alone. Her husband is dead and her kids have grown up and moved away. Hardly anyone stays on the Reservation after they're grown, but I'm going to. I might go away to study art, as Miss Pierce says I should, but I'll come back. I want always to live here in the shadow of my mountain. I wouldn't feel like me anyplace else.

Aunt Ophie is thin and small and she has lively black eyes. Her house isn't neat because she spends all her time making pots and weaving baskets, though she says this is far too much work. Sometimes it takes her weeks, even months, to make one basket, and she's lucky if some rich white person gives her thirty-five dollars for it. Mostly people want to pay only fifteen or twenty dollars. It isn't only the making of the basket that is hard, but Aunt Ophie has to go walking all over to find the right weeds. She calls all plants weeds, waterweeds and squaw-vine weeds. Once when I was little I wanted

to help her so I picked a lot of poison oak instead of squaw-vine. I itched for days.

When I got to Aunt Ophie's house it was lunchtime. Aunt Ophie had a pot of beans on the wood stove and she was making tortillas. The house was nice and warm. She handed me a ball of dough and we stood there, smelling the good beans and patting out tortillas.

I watched Aunt Ophie put the tortillas into a hot dry frying pan one by one, then flip them over with her fingers. A pot of coffee began to boil and she pushed it over to the side of the stove. I was starving by the time we sat down at the kitchen table and started folding our tortillas around beans.

After I swallowed the first mouthful I said, "Our teacher says it is because of the Mexicans that Indians make tortillas."

I had forgotten that Aunt Ophie dislikes Mexicans as much as she does Anglos. "Probably," she said, "*we* showed the Mexicans how to make tortillas."

You can't argue with Aunt Ophie so I changed the subject. "I brought some stuff that might be good clay. Aunt Ophie, will you help me with something?" And I took a deep breath and told her about what I wanted to do.

She kept nodding and saying, "Sure, sure." She promised not to breathe a word about the statue to anyone.

"Do you think that I really can do it, Aunt Ophie?

I know it will be awfully hard and maybe it won't come out right. That's why I don't want anyone to know about it until it is finished."

"Of course you can do it," Aunt Ophie told me. "There's no reason why you can't do anything you want to, if you want to bad enough."

I wondered if this were true and hoped that it was. "Well, I sure *want* to. More than anything else in the whole world."

"Well, do it then," Aunt Ophie said.

I realized that I needed reassurance. Miss Pierce once told us that inspiration is a splendid word but that if you want to make something, you need more than that. You have to work at it, you have to keep trying, even if what you do doesn't seem very good.

I knew that I was willing to work hard. The little coyote on the mountain had shown me that. I just *had* to make the statue.

"My Saint Francis is going to be different from any other," I told Aunt Ophie. "That may be one reason I want to do it so much."

Aunt Ophie nodded. "That's good."

On my way home I climbed to the coyote's ledge again. Aunt Ophie had made too many tortillas for lunch and she'd given me the left-overs to take with me. I hoped that the coyote would like them. I didn't see him, but the food I'd left earlier was gone.

While we were eating supper that night Papa asked, "Well, who is your Aunt Ophie mad at

today?"

Aunt Ophie is my father's very own sister but he is always making fun of her because he says she is a trouble-maker. Every time there is a squabble on the Reservation Aunt Ophie is in it somewhere.

Father Antonio says that he likes a good cold winter because people stay home and don't go around getting into quarrels all the time. He teases us about Indians wanting to go on the warpath, but then again he says that, after all, a reservation is just like any small town anywhere, with the usual number of gossips and scrappers.

Perhaps he is right, but when we have fights we have good ones, sometimes with people throwing rocks and bottles at one another. Fights are exciting and we love excitement.

"I don't think Aunt Ophie's mad at anyone in particular today," I answered Papa. "She's going to help me make pottery out of some clay I found. She's the only one on the whole Reservation who makes pots and baskets any more."

Mama said, "I wonder how many acorns she's got left. Ours are all gone and I want to make some chow-wee."

"I think a lot. I peeked into her big storage basket."

"Acorns always make me think of Grandma," Mama told us. "She'd make the biggest and best storage baskets of anyone and not a drop of rain

41

could get in. In the fall, she was always out gathering acorns, even when she grew so old you wondered how she could walk or see. She used to get mad at us young ones for buying stuff from the store. Grandma saved everything and made the best jerky stew you ever tasted. Everything in it was stuff she'd stored and dried."

Papa laughed. "Even boiled wood rats used to taste good when we were kids."

"Gee," said Teofilo, "I wouldn't want to eat a *rat*."

"But *wood* rats," said Mama. "They're different from old house rats."

Just the same, we didn't like the idea.

Six

THE NEXT day, Sunday, for some reason I woke up
early, before anyone else was up, and I lay there
thinking about the things we'd talked of at the
supper table the night before. I thought about how,
except when tourists are around, we never think that
being Indian is any different from being anything
else. As Mama says, we've been Indians all our lives
and usually we aren't aware of it. When some tourist asks what kind of Indians we are, we say that we
are Mission Indians. Mama read somewhere that
we are descended from the Yumans.

I don't suppose that white people feel it's remarkable to be white people any more than we feel it's
remarkable to be Indian. I wondered about other

43

people, about Negroes and Chinese. I imagine that everyone is just used to being whatever he is.

Then I thought, but we are different. We've been here longer than anyone. Papa said that when the Spaniards first came to California, years and years ago, our people said, "They look like animals with hair all over their faces."

I've heard Papa say that we could have fought off the Spaniards if we hadn't been split into small groups, always fighting among ourselves. In those days, each tribe had its own language so that Indians living only a few miles apart couldn't understand each other. Even today, the Indian language is different on different reservations. This doesn't really matter because none of the young people speak Indian any more. Soon our old languages will be forgotten.

I guess Indians were mean to each other before the white people showed them more meanness. Years ago my mother's great-aunt, who was only a girl then, was stolen by some Indians who came across the desert from Arizona. She happened to be up on the mountain gathering acorns when the Arizona Indians made off with her.

Mama's very own grandmother was sold when she was about my age. An Indian woman wanted her to be her son's wife and she traded twenty-five dollars and an old white horse for her.

So, I thought, we are different, and most of us live

on reservations apart from other people. We still eat acorns even if we don't eat wood rats. When someone dies we usually have a wake, and hired singers and dancers come to it from as far away as Arizona. During the wake we have a mixture of prayers, like in church, some Indian chants and some old Spanish hymns.

We have lots of good things to eat at wakes and funerals. People travel miles from one reservation to another to pay their respects to the dead and to visit with friends they never see except when there is a wake, a funeral, a wedding or a fiesta. Everybody cries very much, but they eat and laugh very much, too.

I remember when my older sister died. I was a very little girl and I cried all during her funeral. Papa cried too, but Mama just looked stunned and odd, as if she didn't really know what was happening.

One other time I saw my father cry.

Before the Indians were chased off the good land and made to go live on the Reservation up on the mountain, my father lived in a pretty little valley with his great-grandmother. He was only a small boy then. His great-grandmother had a good place, with a vegetable garden and a flock of sheep. She certainly didn't want to leave her garden where she had worked so hard and, anyway, this was her home. But the white people wouldn't let her stay there.

Papa helped her round up the sheep and they

walked behind them and drove them up the mountain. Papa says he'll never forget how his great-grandmother cried every step of the way. She cried for days, even after they were settled in a house on the mountain.

Later, she went back to see if she could harvest any of the vegetables she had grown, but cattle had been turned in and her garden was ruined. She didn't go down the mountain any more after that, not until she died. Then the white people let her be buried down in the valley in the Indian graveyard.

A few years ago, the place where she and Papa had lived was made into a boys' camp where city kids came in summer. I remember one time, after Papa had been sick for a couple of days, he decided (I don't know why) that he wanted to go look at his great-grandmother's grave. He came home and cried and went to bed and stayed there for two days.

What had happened was that those city boys had been digging, right in the grave, and hadn't cared in the least that this was a sacred place. They had no right to disturb our dead, but I guess they thought it was fun. Mama said that probably they were looking for arrowheads or pottery or something. Papa didn't cheer up for weeks, and now, remembering about it, I felt sad, too.

That afternoon, after our Sunday dinner, we didn't have any company as we usually have most Sundays. My brothers were off playing with some

kids that live down the canyon and I decided to go look for my coyote.

The day was bright and felt like spring. Higher Than The Arrow looked soft and dreamy, as if spring were already here. There wasn't a single cloud hovering above its peak. I thought about what both Father Antonio and Aunt Ophie had said—that I could do anything I wanted to, if I wanted to do it badly enough. And what I wanted to do most in all the world was to put that coyote into the arms of Saint Francis, to make a truly beautiful statue.

We needed more rain to keep the pasture grass growing and bring out the wildflowers. The rains would come—it wasn't nearly time for the dry season to start. Already the wild lilac had tight purple buds. Miss Pierce says it isn't true lilac at all; I can't remember its real name. It is beautiful when it is all abloom. It makes waves of deep blue and pale blue in the wind and it smells like honey.

It cheered me to think that spring was on the way. I love spring, and next comes summer which I love even more. Summer vacation is great. But before summer we'd have Easter, and I'd have to work hard to get Saint Francis done by then.

All of a sudden I heard hoofbeats behind me. I turned to look, and along came the prettiest, brightest red sorrel I'd ever seen.

I stared at the mare before I noticed her rider. It was Lucy. I was so surprised I kept on staring.

47

"Oh, Francie," Lucy called out, "just look what I got for my birthday. Isn't she beautiful? I named her Redbird."

I couldn't think of a thing to say. I kept on admiring the little mare. She had a white blaze down her face and white socks. I liked the redness of her mane. It was prettier than a flaxen mane, though some people like the contrast. Instead of a saddle Lucy had one of those bareback pads that all the kids want now, and it was a green one. She had a plain russet bridle that was brand-new and looked as suitable to the mare's coloring as the green bareback pad.

Lucy, all happy, smiled down at me. "Well, say something!"

"I can't. What is there to say? She's just beautiful, Lucy. You are so lucky!"

"Aren't I just! This is what I've wanted all my life."

"Me too, but I'm not so lucky." I reached out and patted the mare's glossy neck. "I guess you've been brushing her a lot."

Lucy nodded. "And when she sheds for summer she'll be even brighter. Say, haven't you got a horse? Why can't you ride with me? I've never been on the Reservation before, it's pretty up here. I like the stream. Does it flow all the time?"

"Not in summer, except further up. My dad has a couple of horses, but they're turned out now. Anyway, he doesn't like us kids to ride them. They're

48

good cow horses and he's fussy about them. I ride one sometimes when he goes along too."

"Well, what about those burros I saw? Can you ride one of them?"

"I could, but I don't want to now. I have to go somewhere else."

Lucy sighed. "It'd be fun to have someone to ride with. We could explore."

"I don't need to explore. I know all the trails."

Lucy looked disappointed, so I added, "I can't today. But maybe someday we'll go riding. I've got to go now." I turned and started following the trail to the coyote's ledge.

Seven

On the way home I felt sad because I hadn't seen the coyote. Poor little coyote, perhaps half the time he didn't get the food I left. I felt sorry for him and sorry for me.

I told myself that coyotes and Indians are alike. We are unwanted. I pictured the sorrowful time my people had had when they were driven from their homes. Aunt Ophie says it could happen again if enough real estate people decide to make a resort of our Reservation. Mama just laughs at her, but Papa halfway agrees. He says that city people would love to build cabins up on the Arrow where the pines and incense cedars grow.

If that should happen, we Indians really would be

coyotes. I felt like saying a prayer for all the coyotes in the world, and by coyotes I meant all unhappy people and animals. When I thought that way it made it seem all the better that I had chosen a coyote for Saint Francis to hold.

I had worked myself into a very gloomy state of mind by the time I got home. When I went in the house Papa was taking a nap and Mama was sewing. The boys were still off somewhere.

I must have looked as bad as I felt for Mama glanced up and said, "Why, Francie, whatever is the matter?"

I mumbled that nothing was the matter.

"Nothing whatever," said Mama. "That's why you are wearing a gloom cloud."

"Oh, I was just thinking about things."

"Things? What things?"

"Oh, I don't know. About coyotes and Indians, I guess."

"Coyotes and Indians make you sad? How?"

"We're all the same. Nobody wants us."

"For heaven's sake!" said Mama. "What got you started on all this?"

"I don't know. I was thinking about when Papa found what those boys had done to Great-great-grandmother's grave. And I was thinking about how both coyotes and Indians get shoved around. Things seem sad. And that girl, Lucy Olson . . . Did you see her ride past on that red mare?"

"So *that's* it." Mama looked at me wisely. "But what's it got to do with being Indian? Lots of white kids don't have pretty horses, either."

"Oh, I know. It's not that . . ."

"Well, *what*, then?"

"I don't know . . ."

Mama looked at my perplexed face and laughed. "I wouldn't be your age again for anything! Here you are, all full of moods and whims. What's wrong is—you aren't a little girl any more and you aren't grown-up yet."

"Well, maybe," I said, not knowing whether to agree with her or not.

I went to my room and forced myself to make some sketches, but after a while I gave up.

I kept thinking about Lucy and Redbird out on my mountain. Maybe I admired Lucy more than I realized. Maybe, buried deep, there was a touch of envy.

As the days went on, the air began to smell and taste like spring. There is an excitement about the turning of a season, when things seem to be teetering on the verge. It was as if the whole world was getting ready to roll into spring, and it was starting to roll faster and faster.

School became more of a drag than ever. I wanted to be out on the mountain. Every afternoon, as soon as I got home, I took my sketch pad and some food scraps and went to the coyote's ledge. I hadn't seen

him for days and I didn't know whether he'd been to get his food or whether something else had eaten it. The season might have made him restless, perhaps he was wandering further.

I was restless, too. I wanted so much to make the statue, though now I knew I'd never get it done by Easter. Sometimes I just walked around thinking about it, going to different places on the mountain that I knew and loved. If I didn't see the coyote on his ledge I might see him some place else, or see some other coyote that I could watch.

One afternoon I walked through a narrow draw, came out into meadowland where a few oaks grew, and remembered that I was near what we've always called our magic spring. I went to look at it.

There can't be another spring like it. I went to the edge of the meadow where there was a big flat out-cropping of rock on which I walked as though it were city pavement. Almost in the middle of it lay a thin slab of stone. I pulled it to one side and looked down on my face shining up at me, with blue sky behind it. I wondered who was the first Indian to ever look here and be surprised at himself.

This was me, Francesca Queri, who was going to be an artist, who was going to make a statue of Saint Francis and the coyote.

The water was exactly even with the rock's sur-face. I cupped my hands and had a drink of the sweet water, and, just to watch the magic, I splashed out

handful after handful. The depression full of water is not large, scarcely larger than the potholes the Indian ladies once used for grinding acorns. The spring is no more than a foot wide and how deep it is I guess nobody knows.

I splashed out more water until the level went down several inches, then I watched. Slowly and steadily the water came up, to stop where it always stopped, level with the top of the stone. No matter how wet the winter, the spring has never overflowed. No matter how dry the summer, the water has never dropped below its own level.

We Indians believe that if a sick person drinks water from this spring he's almost sure to get well.

Years ago a boy was very ill, and one night he thought he was dying. He told his mother to fetch water from the spring, he was sure it would make him better. He tried to tell her exactly where to find it.

The poor woman went off to look for it. It was a cold night with an east wind blowing, and she couldn't find the place. A waning moon rose, but even that didn't help and by morning she was so exhausted she could scarcely make her way home. Her clothes were all torn and her face and hands scratched from the brush. The boy had stayed alive all night, waiting for the water, and when she didn't bring it he died. It was especially sad because he was her only one and her husband was dead.

The next day at school Miss Pierce had a talk with me about why I hadn't turned in a drawing for the bulletin board lately. It seemed to bother her that I hadn't.

"What's happening to you, Francie?" she asked. "Is something worrying you?"

"I don't think so," I answered.

"But every week I'd get such a good sketch from you. I've always been proud of your talent. It is a gift you have, Francie, and you don't want to mislay it, do you?"

"Oh, I won't." I hesitated, wondering if I should tell her about my Saint Francis. I decided not to. This had to be a secret because—what if I never got a good statue made? I'd feel silly if I told everyone that I was making a statue and then it turned out wrong. Or, what if people thought I couldn't do it and laughed at the thought that I should get such an idea in the first place? I shut my mouth tight and just looked at Miss Pierce.

"Well, anyway," she said finally, "I know that you wouldn't let it bother you because someone else draws well too. It is your own self that is important. Why, if you want to badly enough, you can go Higher Than The Arrow. Isn't that the name of your wonderful mountain? Do you know what I mean, Francie?"

"Yes, ma'am. I'll make a lot of drawings in Easter vacation."

"How's your sketch pad? Do you need a new one yet?"

"There's still a lot of pages left. I take good care of it and keep it hidden from my brothers and everyone. And I do draw a lot. I go up on the mountain and sketch."

"It must be beautiful up there. You are a lucky girl to have such a mountain and to be able to appreciate it. Some people don't appreciate what they have."

That same afternoon something good happened. The coyote came again. I had climbed to his ledge, put his food down, and was sitting quietly looking across the hills and noticing that they were turning greener every day. Already there was the scent of wild lilac in the air and that made it seem like spring for sure.

My coyote has magic ways of appearing and disappearing. I never see him come; suddenly he is just there. That is the way it was this time. He had stepped out of the brush and may have been looking at me a long time before I saw him.

He was still wearing his winter coat, which had never looked like a nice thick, smooth one, and now, ready to shed, it was all rough and patchy. But it was a good brown, woodsy color. It was too shaggy for me to tell whether or not he was very thin.

Certain kinds of dogs sometimes seem to look like coyotes, but when you see a real coyote you realize that even the most coyote-looking dog doesn't match

up. A coyote's face is far more delicate and sharp. Also, he has alertness that no domestic animal has. His ears are extra-triangular.

Now, as I watched, my coyote did the most appealing thing, though when I tell it, it doesn't sound like much. He sat down and scratched an ear with one hind foot, just as Jack does. To me it was wonderful because, for that one second, he was not on guard against me. He was doing something natural, the sort of thing he would do when he was all by himself. He was scratching an ear, as if I weren't there at all.

Then he stood up, shook himself, and disappeared. I continued to hold still because I felt that he was watching me from behind a clump of bushes.

People are always watching birds and deer and other creatures, never knowing how many animals may be watching them. There are bird-watchers and there are people-watchers. Coyotes and foxes and other curious ones are surely people-watchers.

After a while I tried making a sketch of a coyote scratching his ear. It was difficult and my first tries turned out to be stiff and unreal-looking. But finally it came easier and all of a sudden my pencil wouldn't make a wrong line. It is perfectly lovely when sketching goes like that.

I knew that here was a picture Miss Pierce would like. She did. It was my coyote that was the next picture to go up on the bulletin board.

Eight

THE OTHER day we got out of school earlier than usual because there was going to be a teachers' meeting. We hadn't been home very long before Lucy came riding along on Redbird. She rode right into our yard and Jack started barking. We all looked out the window.

"Francie," Lucy called. "Come on out."

I opened the window. "I can't. I have to help my mother."

Mama said, "That's all right. Go talk to your friend."

"I don't want to."

By then Teofilo and Jerry were outside making a big fuss over the mare. You'd think they'd never

seen any kind of horse before.

I drew back from the window so that I could watch without being seen. My mouth fell open when Lucy got off Redbird and Teofilo got on her and rode her around the yard. Then it was Jerry's turn.

After that, they all stood around talking, then the boys hurried to the shed and came back with ropes. So they were going to ride the burros. We had seen the three animals grazing along the road when Mama brought us home from the school bus, so they couldn't be very far away.

Pretty soon they all rode off. Lucy had let Teofilo ride the mare again, and she was jogging along on a burro and giggling. The third burro heehawed because he didn't like being left alone, and went loping after them. Even Jack, looking happy, ran along beside them.

"Now why didn't you go?" asked Mama. "You could have had fun."

I shrugged. "I don't know. I didn't feel like it."

I really would liked to have gone, but I wanted to think about the loving-kindness of Saint Francis and the sadness of coyotes. I wanted to go up to the ledge and be quiet, perhaps see my coyote.

Lucy would think that I was unfriendly, but I couldn't help it. When you want to do something as much as I want to make that statue you just can't let other things get in your way. Even if it does make you feel a little lonely.

I thought the young coyote must be lonely too. And hungry.

I climbed up to the ledge, put down the food I had brought, and went to my usual place to wait. I practiced holding very still, the way animals do when they don't want to be seen. Papa once told us about a big buck deer that didn't go crashing off through the brush when he heard people; instead, he just waited, still as a statue, in a spot where his coloring matched his background. Papa said that the only reason he'd been able to see him was that his horse would scent him or glimpse him, then stop and prick up his ears. Anyone not riding a smart horse never would have seen him.

I hoped that my coyote would learn to be that careful and not let himself get shot at. Then I thought of something worse—traps. The thought made me a little sick. Where was there any safety for a coyote?

I kept wishing I'd see him. He must have been a dear small pup when he lived in the den with his mother and the other pups. Perhaps there had been three of them, all warm and soft and full of milk. Probably their mother had bathed them a lot, the way mother dogs do. And when they were old enough she'd have brought them rabbits and squirrels and mice. No doubt then they'd all started to fight, each wanting the most to eat. I wondered if the father coyote had helped hunt food for the pups.

61

Papa says that coyotes keep their same mates and grow fond of each other.

Once Papa happened to see three coyote pups playing outside their den. They played like little dogs, he said, wrestling and biting and growling. One was running around with a small stick in his mouth. It was his plaything. I thought about how much I would love to see something like that. I'd like to have a tiny coyote to raise, but I wouldn't want to steal one from its mother.

Though I stayed on the ledge a long time, the coyote didn't come.

As I started to climb down, I happened to look across the canyon. There, riding down a slope, were my brothers and Lucy. Where had they been, I wondered. They were laughing and talking as if they were having a fine time, though I couldn't hear what they were saying.

I felt strange and left out, even though I knew I could have been with them had I chosen.

They disappeared without seeing me and I went on down the canyon trail. Then I did a strange thing. Instead of walking on toward home, I went up the slope, backtracking mare and burros. Suddenly, with a feeling of annoyance, I was sure I knew where those three had been. I left their trail to take a short-cut I knew, hurried up a narrow draw, and came to the meadow and the outcropping of stone.

Shining like glass was the magic spring. They

hadn't even bothered to put back its stone cover!

I was furious. I was furious because Jerry and Teofilo had shown our spring to a white girl and I was furious at the carelessness of all of them.

I caught sight of my face as I bent down to shove the stone into place. It caught me unawares and I stared. So this was how I looked when my face was all hard and dark with anger!

When I got home Jerry and Teofilo were there, the burros turned loose, and Lucy was gone. Mama was cooking supper and I had to set the table.

Jerry said, "You should have come, we had fun."

Teofilo said, "We showed Lucy the magic spring."

"Oh!" I banged down a plate so hard it nearly cracked. "Well, you shouldn't have."

"For gosh sakes, why not?"

"You know why as well as I do."

Mama said, "Oh, what does it matter? Come dish up the beans now."

Jerry had another piece of information to offer. "We saw a coyote. Looked like the same one we saw the day we went to find clay. He crossed the trail right below that ledge. He got scared when Teofilo yelled at him and he went the other way."

I really was mad then. They'd frightened my coyote just when I'd been waiting to see him. Probably he hadn't even gone for the food I'd left.

"Oh!" I shouted. "How dumb can you be! Stupid idiots! Scare my coyote and then show that girl the

spring and tell her all about it! Haven't you got a brain between the two of you?"

"What do you mean, *your* coyote?" Teofilo yelled. "You don't make sense."

I wanted to hit him, but Papa intervened.

"Oh, quiet down. I swear you're getting more like your Aunt Ophie every day, Francie. What are you so excited about anyhow?"

So I didn't say any more. But I didn't stop being mad.

Nine

By the next morning I could wonder why it had made me so angry that the boys had shown our secret spring to Lucy. After all, I thought, Lucy wouldn't understand about it anyway. Perhaps it was really myself I was mad at. A frustrated artist is terrible. Here I'd thought I was going to have a wonderful statue all made by Easter and I hadn't even started it.

But about the boys scaring the coyote, I was still infuriated. I wouldn't speak to them as Mama drove us to the school bus. Not that it did them any good. Half the time brothers are too stupid to know why you are mad.

At school, when Lucy and I had a chance to talk, she said, "You should have been along yesterday,

65

we had fun."

"I couldn't go. I had something else to do."

As I looked at Lucy I had a surprising thought. She was certainly acting as if she really truly wanted me for a friend. I stared at her, standing there in a blue-and-white dress, her eyes as blue as the dress itself. I gulped and said, "I'll go along when I can."

Why me, I wondered. All the kids seemed to like Lucy, she could have as many friends as she wanted. And I couldn't understand why she put up with Teofilo and Jerry. Maybe because she didn't have any brothers of her own.

I decided I wouldn't encourage her or discourage her. I'd just wait and see what happened. If I were to give my friendship to someone it would be a big thing to me. So I wasn't going to be in a hurry. Then I wondered if, without realizing it, I was being influenced by Aunt Ophie's opinions about white people. Could it be that I wouldn't trust a white girl as a friend?

Maybe I was resentful because Lucy was a good artist. Or had that business about our secret spring prejudiced me because I didn't think white people should know about it? I wondered if I really were going to grow up to be like Aunt Ophie.

That next Saturday I took a shovel and a feed sack to the spot on the coyote's ledge where we'd found the red earth. I planned to dig some to take to Aunt Ophie's. She'd show me how to start working it.

I dug up a great lot of earth and carried it down to the road. The rains had kept the canyon stream going, only now it was clear and not running fast. It sparkled and splashed over the rocks and I enjoyed having it beside me as I walked along.

Suddenly I heard a patter of hoofs behind me. Along the road came Lucy on Redbird, Teofilo and Jerry on the burros, the third burro tagging along.

All of them stopped and Lucy said, "Why don't you jump on the other burro and come with us?"

"What's that you've got?" Jerry wanted to know.

"Clay for Aunt Ophie. I've got to go there."

"You ought to come with us. We're going to look for arrowheads and pieces of pottery."

Teofilo said, "Maybe we'll find a whole unbroken *olla* in the rocks."

"I bet you won't. The Indians were smart about where they hid them." I turned and walked on.

"I wish you could come," Lucy called after me.

They jogged on ahead of me and disappeared around a bend in the road.

I found Aunt Ophie outside, washing clothes. "I saw your brothers go by with that girl," she said. She sniffed as she said it, the way she does when she disapproves of someone.

I shrugged. "They think they're going to find some arrowheads or something. Aunt Ophie, is this good clay? Can you show me how to work it? Remember what I told you about making a statue of

Saint Francis?"

Aunt Ophie squeezed a lump and said it was good enough, though it would have to be cleaned before we could really do anything with it. Suddenly, like magic, she made a little clay bird.

So then I tried making one, only mine wasn't as good as Aunt Ophie's.

"There's on old story that when Our Lord was a little boy He was outdoors playing with mud," Aunt Ophie said after a while. "He made little birds and blew on them, and they came alive and flew away."

"Oh," I exclaimed, "I never heard that one. I wonder if He made a few coyotes, too."

"Now why would He do that?" Aunt Ophie wanted to know. "They probably didn't have any coyotes in the Holy Land anyway."

"I suppose Saint Francis never saw a coyote?"

"So far as I know, he didn't."

"But I bet he'd have liked one if he saw it. He loved everything that God made."

"Even rattlesnakes?" Aunt Ophie asked.

"I suppose he never saw one of those either."

"Well, who knows? Now you help me hang out these clothes and then we'll have some beans and tortillas. Afterward, we'll fool with the clay some more."

After we finished lunch Aunt Ophie took the clay and dumped it onto a cloth. "It's still good and wet. If it was dry we could pound it on a big rock and

sift it. It's all right to have lots of tiny gravel left in. That helps when we fire it."

I watched as Aunt Ophie poked the clay with her fingers. She stared at it earnestly. I stared at it too. Here was a big hunk of red earthy clay, and it was going to become something more.

"First you have to look and look," Aunt Ophie explained. "If I make a pot I look a long time at the clay to see if maybe a pot is in there."

I stared at the clay to see if Saint Francis could be there, and the more I stared the more excited I became.

Aunt Ophie took my right hand and looked at my thumb. "Good. You need a flat thumb, sort of like a little foot."

She got out a tin tub and put the clay into it. After she'd covered it with water she handed me a sawed-off broomstick. "Now you stir and stir and pound and pound. Work it and work it."

I kept at it, and when my arms and shoulders began to ache Aunt Ophie took over for a while. At last, we could pour off the water, and then Aunt Ophie showed me how to work the clay through a sieve.

"When it dries to the right feeling, then you knead it like bread."

On the way home I was almost too tired to climb up and leave some tortillas for the coyote but I did it anyway.

Teofilo and Jerry were all excited about the day they'd had with Lucy, though they hadn't found any Indian relics. Lucy had told them that she'd heard or read that there might be treasures on our mountain. "All sorts of gold chalices and things from the missions in Lower California," Teofilo told Papa. "They had to hide things when the government changed and made some new laws."

"Is that so?" said Papa.

I was too tired to listen and I went to bed early. I'd had a very happy day.

Ten

AT SCHOOL on Monday we had a math test. Miss
Pierce had started us on the beginning of algebra
because she thought it might help when we got into
high school. None of it made the slightest sense to
me.

When Mama and Papa were little they had gone
to school out under an oak tree and I thought about
how I'd have liked that. After the tree school stopped,
because the lady who taught the kids moved away,
Mama was sent off to Indian school. She said she
was awfully homesick at first, but then she found a
friend, a girl named Belinda. Belinda and Mama got
to be very best friends. A best friend would sure be
a good thing to have.

I couldn't keep my mind on the algebra problems. I didn't care two hoots what "x" was. I thought of Mama, starting off to Indian school in a wagon drawn by two horses, and I thought I would have liked that part. But Mama had cried all the way.

With spring outside, about to light up the whole mountain with flowers and streams, it was awful to stay indoors. Instead of concentrating on the test, I began to make sketches of my coyote. I made one of a paw, one of an ear, one of his muzzle. Then I made a beautiful bushy coyote tail.

Suddenly Miss Pierce said, "Time's up. Turn in your papers, class."

I guess I must have groaned out loud because several kids giggled. Miss Pierce gave me the kind of look she gives me sometimes. It's a look that says, "Francie, I'm disappointed in you."

I glanced at Lucy and felt that she too was laughing at me. I stared out the window. I could see a part of a pasture, one tree, and a piece of sky.

I knew that after Miss Pierce saw I hadn't finished the algebra test she'd ask me to stop for a minute after school. She did. But she didn't say much. Only that just because I was a good artist didn't mean that I shouldn't try to do well at other things. She looked at me and sighed. "There is no reason why you can't be an excellent student, Francie."

When we got on the bus to go home Lucy came and sat beside me. I thought, she wants to be nice

to me, she feels sorry for me, and that annoyed me all the more. I didn't offer any conversation and when Lucy made remarks I answered her briefly.

As soon as I got home I changed my clothes as quickly as I could. As I started out for the mountain, Mama called after me, "Why don't you dust up your room? It's looking terrible again."

Even Mama didn't know that I had more important things to do.

Someday I'd show them, I thought, as I hurried along with food for my coyote. That coyote and I had a secret, even if the coyote didn't know it.

He had eaten yesterday's food. And I saw his paw prints in some soft earth. That pleased me, even if I didn't see him. At least I knew he was still all right.

As I was going home, I ran into my brothers on the burros and Lucy on Redbird.

"We're going to look at some potholes," Jerry said.

Lucy said, "Come with us this time. You never do."

"I haven't got a rope."

"Here, use my tie-rope," Lucy offered.

So I caught the third burro, who was going along because he wouldn't be left alone. I twisted a loop around his nose and jumped on his back.

Teofilo led the way up a little grassy draw until we were in a small meadow where there was a flat slab of rock. In the rock were seven potholes, deep and

worn.

"See," he said, "the Indian ladies used these to grind acorns in. They had a good view all around, too, and if they saw anyone they didn't like they could hide in the brush real quick."

"We don't use potholes any more," Jerry explained. "Mama has a *metate* she uses instead."

Lucy was interested. "You still eat acorns?"

Jerry said, "Of course. Next time Mama makes some acorn mush we'll give you some."

"And she really grinds acorns in a *metate*? Down at the ranch we have some in the garden, someone found them and put them there. Big stones with hollows worn in them. They must be very old."

Teofilo found some pieces of broken pottery by the edge of the rock. Jerry picked up a smooth stone. "See, this is a pestle. The thing they used to grind with."

Lucy got off Redbird and put her hand down into a pothole. "How smooth and worn it is. I wonder what the Indian ladies talked about when they sat here."

"Oh," Teofilo said, "probably about their husbands and kids. And who was good and who was bad. Lots of gossip, I bet."

"Well, after all," said Lucy, "they were *people*."

"Well, what would you expect them to be? Don't you think we're people?" I blurted out. As soon as I'd said it I wished I hadn't. It was a stupid thing to

74

say, but the words had come out before I'd thought.

"For-crying-out-loud! Lucy turned and got back on the mare. She looked angry. "We better go home, it's getting late."

As we rode down the shadowed hills I kept wishing I could think of some way to smooth things over. I didn't know what to say, so I kept still. I was annoyed at myself for spoiling the good time we'd been having. And why should it matter, anyway, that my brothers kept showing Indian things to a white girl?

Eleven

Just before Easter vacation Miss Pierce made an announcement to the class. "When school takes up again," she said, "it will be time to start getting ready for our annual exhibit for parents which we have at the end of the school year. So, in art period, we're going to start working in clay. I thought it would be fun to try to produce some clay figures for the exhibit this time, instead of just showing the best drawings from the class. Would you all like that?"

I could scarcely believe my ears. Little did Miss Pierce know that I was already working in clay. Then a thought struck me. Of course—I could show my Saint Francis in the exhibit and the parents of all the kids in school would come to admire it. How sur-

prised everybody would be! I guess my "yes" was the loudest one of all as we answered Miss Pierce.

Lucy had said a good loud "yes," too. She had acted huffy for a time after I'd made that remark at the potholes, but her huff had worn off. I'd sort of halfway apologized, but not in words. I'd acted just ordinarily friendly toward her, as if I didn't know that I'd said anything to make her mad.

I love Easter time. It comes at the most beautiful season of the year, with grass green, streams flowing, wild lilacs on the hills. Soon new calves and colts would come to the pastures. This Easter vacation had the grass and the streams and the lilacs and all the good smells, but it turned cold and cloudy. Then it began to rain.

Papa was pleased because he likes lots of rain to fill the springs and wells and water the pasture grass. But Teofilo and Jerry and I didn't like it one bit. We thought it ought to rain during school days and stay sunny during vacation.

I hoped that my little coyote would find a dry place to hide. I would manage to continue leaving food on his ledge, rain or no rain. I had decided what I'd do this vacation. I'd spend all the time I could at Aunt Ophie's and work with the clay. When we went back to school I'd be way ahead of the other kids.

By Monday morning Mama was glad to get us out of the house. It had rained all of Palm Sunday, though we had gotten to church, and it rained hard

all that night. In the morning there were clouds moving darkly all over the sky, but it wasn't raining, only misting a little from time to time.

There were watery sounds everywhere. Rivulets poured off the mountain, the canyon stream was roaring. Mama gave up trying to keep us indoors and the boys went out to play in the water and to see if there were big waterfalls farther up the canyon.

I told Mama I wanted to go visit Aunt Ophie and she thought that was a good idea. I bundled up and took some food to leave for the coyote.

I got good and wet from the brush when I climbed to the ledge. After I was on Aunt Ophie's road I had to hurry to keep warm. Clouds moved and I looked up to see snow on Higher Than The Arrow. Ordinarily, you wouldn't expect snow so near to Easter, but there it was. I stopped and stared at it until a thick cloud settled over its peak.

But during that brief interval of seeing the white tip of the Arrow, a thought had come into my head. There was no reason, no reason at all, why I couldn't go ahead and really and truly make my statue during this vacation. I'd spent hours thinking and dreaming about it, picturing how it should look. I'd made dozens of sketches. But I'd wasted time being exasperated at people and things. Maybe, up to now, I'd been afraid to actually start work. Perhaps secretly I had feared I couldn't make it turn out the way I wanted it to.

Perhaps, in my mind, the statue had been clouded as the mountain was now. But behind the cloud there was the mountain. Behind my doubt there was the statue.

I felt more and more elated as I hurried along. Of course I could make a perfect statue! I was the best artist in our entire school. Lucy was good, but I was better.

By the time I reached Aunt Ophie's my heart was pounding. I burst through the door, and before she could tell me to take off my wet coat and shoes, I was telling her about how we were going to make clay things at school, and how I was going to make my statue in vacation and be way ahead of everyone else.

"Sure. Why not?" Aunt Ophie said calmly.

"I want to start work now, right this minute. And I'll come back every day and work some more. You'll help me, won't you, Aunt Ophie?"

"Sure. Here, put your coat by the stove. And take off those wet shoes."

So we went to work, Aunt Ophie and I. And now I didn't have a doubt in my head. Saint Francis and the coyote were going to be perfect.

Twelve

My ENTHUSIASM carried me along, and it carried Aunt Ophie along, too. "That teacher, she'll find out. An Indian girl can do anything."

But it wasn't easy.

First we made a little flat piece of clay for the base of the statue. It was like a plate with a hole in it. I hadn't even known that the statue must be hollow inside, because otherwise it couldn't be fired.

Aunt Ophie showed me how to roll out coils of clay so that, at the very beginning, it seemed I was going to make a snake. The coils went around and around, one on top of another. The inside must be smoothed, the outside smoothed and shaped. We could go only so far before we had to stop and let the

clay set until the next day.

Aunt Ophie had tools we could use—two flattish, smooth stones and little strong, sharp sticks. These smoothing stones may have been used for hundreds of years, Aunt Ophie said. She had inherited them from her mother who had inherited them from her mother. Aunt Ophie said you can find such stones wherever Indians have lived. "When you find one that feels right in your hand you must never lose it," she told me. "I couldn't work without these."

But she explained that it was the work of the hands that was important, that I mustn't use the tools until my fingers had done all the work they possibly could. "Your hands must make the clay have the life. When you get it as smooth as you can, then you can use the stones. And these sticks will make eyes and lines in the face, and the coyote hair. Why you want to make a coyote I'll never know," she added.

I smoothed up and down as I went along and sometimes there came a close feeling between my fingers and the clay. At other times it would seem as if the clay itself were being stubborn. When that happened, I'd stop and study all the sketches I had made.

When the work went well I felt joyful inside. Where there had been nothing, something was appearing. Into empty space came something made of earth. And I thought how Saint Francis loved the earth and all on it and how it was good to make his

82

figure from the earth.

But there were problems. I had wanted the coyote to hang limply in the saint's arms, his paws dangling. This made for a lot of detail and the paws could easily break off. Finally I found that I had to mould the coyote tight against Saint Francis's robe. Not even an ear would stick up by itself. I found that it was difficult, too, to put any expression into the clay face. Expression had to be in the posture of the body. Saint Francis could bend slightly over the animal, his eyes could be looking down, with eyelids dropped.

My enthusiasm kept up. In bed at night I'd keep thinking about how beautiful the statue was going to be and how I'd astonish people like Miss Pierce and Father Antonio and even Mama. All the kids, especially Lucy, would be surprised too.

Aunt Ophie wanted me to spend the whole vacation week at her house on account of the rain, but I wouldn't. Though the weather stayed wet, it didn't rain every minute and I could set out for Aunt Ophie's between showers. I wanted to take food to the coyote each day. I didn't once see him, or even his tracks, but the food was always gone. Of course I couldn't be sure that birds or squirrels hadn't found it before he had. I could only hope.

Mama was good about letting me go off. She thought Aunt Ophie and I were making pottery.

For the first day or two, nothing went very well.

I was ready to squash the lump of clay and start over again, but Aunt Ophie showed me how you just have to keep on pressing and smoothing, a little bit at a time. But often I worked for a couple of hours without seeing any real progress.

Once Aunt Ophie said, "That statue's got to be all good from inside out so that when you fire it it'll come out right. No air bubbles."

This scared me. "You mean it can go wrong when we fire it?"

"Oh, yes. I busted lots of pots that way."

"Aunt Ophie, it can't! It just *can't!* The statue has to be perfect."

"Don't worry. We'd do it over again."

"I couldn't bear to. This has got to be it."

"Anyway, it'll be a long time before we can fire it. All the oak wood and cow chips and everything are too wet to build a fire with now."

By the end of the week it was like "Ready or not, here I come." My statue had to be finished.

And it was. Aunt Ophie and I stood back to look at it, and if she felt any misgivings she didn't say so. I thought that it was as beautiful as it could be before it was fired and painted. Saint Francis, of course, must wear a brown robe. His sun-beaten face would be the color of our faces. The coyote would very nearly match the saint's robe. That robe had been a great help, both in the moulding of the figure and because I had made it long enough so that there was

no need to show sandaled feet, which would have been too hard to do. I had had fun making a braided cord around Saint Francis's waist. This detail was more enjoyable to do than the lumpy stuff, more like sketching.

I sighed with delight.

"Now what?" asked Aunt Ophie. "Perhaps you better leave it here until we can fire it."

"No," I decided, "I'll wrap it up in a gunnysack and take it home. I'll hide it under my bed. Then I'll have it in case I get a sudden idea and want to do more work."

"You'll have to keep it damp for a few days. I'll sprinkle some water on it and wrap it up. Carry it very carefully."

As I started home, the rain seemed to be all over. Only around the edges of the sky were there clouds and in the west the sun was turning them gold. I looked up to the snow on Higher Than The Arrow and it was reflecting gold too.

Thirteen

BACK AT school that first day, I could scarcely wait until art period. But we had a disappointment. Miss Pierce told us that the clay which had been ordered for our class hadn't come yet. She told us to go ahead and make sketches of whatever we wanted to model. She said to use our imaginations and choose whatever subject we liked.

I thought I'd had enough of sketching and I wasn't enthused as I worked away at a drawing of a coyote.

Now that we were in school the weather was beautiful and sunny. It would have been exasperating except that I'd accomplished so much during that rainy week.

I'd continued to keep the statue hidden under my

bed. It was odd, perhaps, that I didn't want to keep looking at it all the time, but I didn't. I just liked to think of it the way it was, perfectly beautiful.

By Thursday the sky was dark again, ready for a new storm. And that day the clay arrived. Everybody was delighted to have something new to do and began trying to make all sorts of things. Miss Pierce said to go ahead and experiment until we got the feel of the material.

Lucy started making a calf, which surprised me. I would have thought she'd try to make a model of Redbird. A few of the kids were trying to do horses, and one boy was making a pig, which I thought was easier and a good idea.

I began modeling a coyote.

Before the period was over Lucy's calf was so good that Miss Pierce held it up for everyone to admire. It was a dear little calf, new and spraddly-legged. Miss Pierce said, "Lucy, this is very good indeed."

Lucy looked pleased. "Where I went to school before, we worked in clay a lot. So I got kind of used to it," she said modestly.

"Your technique is *very* good," Miss Pierce told her. "Excellent, in fact."

She didn't say anything about my coyote, but then, he wasn't nearly finished.

I kept thinking, Miss Pierce would sure be surprised if she knew I'd made a whole beautiful statue. Suddenly I thought, I ought to show it to her now,

even before it's all finished.

I guess I wanted a little praise for myself. I was used to being praised. It wasn't that I begrudged Lucy, but I wanted it known that I was good, too.

The idea kept plaguing me and by the next morning, which was Friday, I'd decided to take the statue to school to show Miss Pierce. Everyone would be asking me what I was carrying, all wrapped up, and I'd tell them it was none of their business. If Mama got curious, I'd say it was a surprise and that she'd find out later. Mama understands about secrets.

It hadn't rained yet but the sky was black and it was unusually cold. I tried to carry the statue under my coat. No one, except my brothers, acted very nosey. As soon as we reached school, before the first bell rang, I waited outside the teacher's lounge for Miss Pierce to come out.

Fortunately, she came out alone. "Miss Pierce, I have something I want to show you—later, maybe during recess. But I haven't any safe place to put it. Could you hide it in your car? Would it be safe?"

"Why, Francie, how interesting! What is it? Something you've made?"

"Yes, and I'm dying to show it to you. But there isn't time now."

"I'll put it in a good place," she promised. "I can hardly wait to see it."

I couldn't wait either. Time dragged until recess. By then it was so cold that no one wanted to go out-

side, but Miss Pierce shooed the kids out anyway and told them to run around to keep warm.

Then she turned to me. "I'll get your package."

She came back with the statue and put it down on her desk. My hands shook as I unwrapped it. What if it wasn't as beautiful as I thought it to be?

Miss Pierce gasped. "Why, Francie! Saint Francis and—what is this? A coyote! Why, what a beautiful, *beautiful* idea! Who but you would think of it? Probably no one in the world ever made a Saint Francis holding a coyote!"

I trembled with joy. "Let's put it away again. I don't want anyone else to see it until it is fired and all painted."

I was so pleased at Miss Pierce's reaction that during art period that morning I really went to work on the coyote I'd only half-heartedly started to model the day before. Lucy put the finishing touches on her calf and everyone admired it all over again. Miss Pierce didn't say anything about my coyote, but she didn't have to.

Just before the lunch hour Miss Pierce said, "Lucy, can you and Francie wait a minute? I want to talk to you about something. I won't keep you long."

The bell rang and the rest of the kids rushed out. Miss Pierce said, "Francie, do you mind if I show Lucy your secret? I'd love to talk to both of you about it."

By then I was so eager for more admiration that I

nodded emphatically. Miss Pierce brought the statue and let me unwrap it.

Lucy's blue eyes grew enormously big. "A coyote! Francie, what a great idea!"

"Isn't it!" Miss Pierce agreed. "It can be the best thing in the whole school exhibit. And Lucy, your technique is so splendid. See what it needs here?"

Lucy nodded and Miss Pierce went on, "It just came to me suddenly how wonderful it would be if you helped Francie with this. She has the idea and the feeling, you have the know-how."

It took me several seconds to get it through my head that I wasn't getting praise. I was getting criticism. For a time I felt completely numb. I stared out the window at the cold dark sky. I listened, without hearing, to Miss Pierce and Lucy. Nothing seemed real.

"Francie, are you paying attention? We must talk this over a little more. Why don't you both wait after school? There'll be time to discuss this before the bus leaves . . . Francie, whatever is the matter?"

How could I tell them what was the matter? How could I explain what I felt? My hands did not seem like my own as I reached out, covered my statue, snatched it up.

"*Thank you very much.* I need no help from Miss Lucy Olson or anyone else." I started for the door.

Miss Pierce cried, "Francie, wait. I didn't mean . . . Francie, you and Lucy see me after school. We must

91

talk this out."

I turned around. Lucy was staring at me as if she were torn between astonishment and anger. "Francie, what's wrong with you?"

"Nothing's wrong with *me*," I cried. "But there's plenty wrong with *you*. What do *you* know about Saint Francis and coyotes and things? What do you know about anything?"

Lucy was trembling now. "I know what's wrong with you," she shouted back. "You're an idiot. A conceited, stupid idiot. I hate you!"

"Girls! Stop! Listen to me!"

But I wouldn't listen. I rushed away. I didn't want to see Lucy or Miss Pierce ever again.

I don't know what Lucy did with her lunch period, but I ran off. Clutching my statue so tightly I must have squeezed it out of shape, I ran across the road, ducked under a fence and kept going. Where the creek bed in the pasture makes a curve there is a cottonwood, old and big and twisted. *Alamo*, the Mexican kids call it. Now it was bare. Last fall all its gold shimmering leaves had fallen to the ground. Dead and brown, they were deep as I scuffed into them.

With my hands I dug a depression and in it I put Saint Francis and the coyote. I didn't even unwrap the statue. I couldn't bear to look. I covered it completely with the leaves. It was awful. It was as if my coyote were dead and I had buried him.

92

I'm strange, I guess, about trees and rocks and things. Even if this tree was having its winter sleep, it was alive, old, and somehow wise. I put my arms around the big trunk, as far as they would go, and then I let myself cry.

But not for long. The lunch period must be over. I felt as if going back into that schoolroom was the worst thing in the world to do, but I was afraid not to. Someone might have seen me run across the road. If I were not there after the bell rang, Miss Pierce would surely send after me and this I could not endure.

Though the air was freezing cold, my face felt hot. My eyes burned. I crept down to the creek and splashed water on my face with both hands. I made myself hold my eyes open and washed out all the tears. Probably I looked better then, but I didn't feel any better. I wanted to stay there all afternoon and let the old tree comfort me.

It was torture, but I walked back across the pasture in time to troop in with the other kids when the bell rang. I didn't look at anyone. I sat at my desk, my head bent over a book. But instead of feeling sorrowful, I found I was growing more and more angry. The nerve of Lucy to think she could work on *my* Saint Francis statute. I remembered how I had felt when the boys showed Lucy our secret spring. I remembered the silly things she'd said that day when we'd been looking at the potholes. I thought how

smug she was, how self-satisfied.

Thank goodness Miss Pierce had sense enough to leave me alone all that long afternoon. She didn't call on me once. In fact, she didn't seem to notice that I was there. I kept staring at the open book in front of me and never once lifted my head to see anything else.

There was one thing I knew for sure. I was *not* going to meet with Miss Pierce and Lucy after school. They could wait for me all night if they wanted to.

As soon as school was over I rushed to the cloak-room, grabbed my coat, and ran to the girls' room. I shut myself in. I'd wait until the bus carted Lucy off, then I'd hitchhike home. By now any tears I shed were those of pure anger.

After I heard the bus leave I waited longer, giving Miss Pierce plenty of time to get to her car and drive away. At last I thought I'd better go before they locked up the school with me in it.

Outside, a few drops of cold rain fell as I hurried along the highway. I rounded the first bend—and there was Lucy, walking ahead of me. She and Miss Pierce must have waited so long for me that she'd missed the bus. Not wanting to catch up with her, I slowed, hoping she wouldn't see me. Suddenly the rain turned to small, hard flakes of snow that stung against my face. A sharp wind swirled them around. They pelted so fiercely and so fast that it was difficult to see very far.

A car came along and stopped. There was a man and a lady in the front seat. The lady put down her window and called, "Jump in. We can drop you off where you want to go."

Mama had always told me not to get into a car with strangers, but this was different. I scrambled in and explained that I'd missed the bus.

In a minute the lady said, surprised, "Here's another little girl." The man stopped the car. Lucy hesitated when she saw me and I thought for a second she wasn't going to get in. The lady said, "Hurry, it's freezing cold." Then Lucy was sitting beside me on the back seat.

I didn't say one word. Lucy and the people in the front seat made some polite remarks about the weather. The man drove slowly, trying to see.

To this day I don't know what evil thing got into me. After we'd gone some miles I said quickly, before I could change my mind, "You can let us out here."

Lucy looked at me with surprise.

"Oh, no," the lady said, "you can't get out here in this storm. I don't see any houses or anything."

"It's all right, really it is. I know where we are, nearly home. I know a shortcut. Come on Lucy, your mother is going to worry if you don't hurry home."

The man said, "Are you sure?"

"Yes, sir. I was raised here. I've seen worse snows than this. Anyway, your car couldn't get up the

Reservation road where I live."

"Well . . ." Reluctantly, he slowed to a stop.

Lucy got out of the car and stood shivering, looking around here uncertainly. "I don't even know where we are," she said as the car drove off.

"Well, I do. Can you see those two trees over there? A trail goes along behind them. You go over a little tiny hill and you're home."

"I can't see any hill. I can hardly see the trees."

"Of course you can't from here. You can't see far ahead in the snow. But you'll see it when you come to it—just a little knoll, and right on the other side is your house. You better hurry." I turned and started running away from her. I slipped and nearly fell.

I looked back, but the snow was so thick by now that I couldn't see Lucy. In my heart I knew it was wrong, but I hoped I'd never see her again. The way I'd told her to go wasn't the way at all—and I was glad.

Mama was mad at me and mad at the boys when at last, numb and half-frozen, I reached our house. "You've certainly worried Papa and me. Why were you so stupid you missed the bus?"

"Because the stupid teacher wanted to talk to me."

"And you boys! Why didn't you tell the driver to wait for your sister? What's the matter with you, anyway?"

"Aw, we didn't know she hadn't got on. She usu-

ally sits in the back."

"You did too know and you didn't care," I stormed. I was glad for an excuse to be mad at the boys.

"That bus driver, he should know how many kids he's got to carry," Papa said. "Somebody ought to tell him a thing or two."

"We were just about to start out to look for you," Mama added.

The wind had risen. It screamed and howled around the house and came in through the cracks. Papa put more wood in the stove. By the time supper was ready I found I couldn't eat. All my anger had been replaced by fear.

As it turned out, no one had any supper. We heard, above the sound of the wind, someone pounding on the door. Papa went to open it. A man's voice said, "The little Olson girl is lost. Can you help us look for her?"

The boys jumped up and started pulling on their coats and I hurried to get mine. Mama said, "No you don't, Francie. You stay right here."

I began to cry. *I* had done this thing. At that moment I would have given anything in the world if I hadn't yielded to that awful impulse there in the car. If only you could go back and fix the wrong thing right, I thought. But you never can. Once anything is said or done, it is forever too late to repair it. I was sick at myself. I wanted to run out in the snow

and die.

"It isn't that bad a storm. They'll find her soon," Mama tried to comfort me. "Stop crying, Francie. Be sensible."

But for me there was no comfort.

Fourteen

I sat by the stove. It was warm in the house but I still shivered. I thought of Lucy, out in the cold and the dark. Mama told me to go to bed, but I couldn't.

I thought how my dream of Saint Francis and the coyote was forever spoiled and how, if it hadn't been for the statue, Lucy wouldn't be out there, lost and cold. Maybe dead. I began to sob again.

Mama said, "They'll find her, Francie. Don't take it so hard."

I thought, "My own mother would hate me if she knew what I'd done." I kept on crying.

It seemed forever before the door opened and Papa and the boys came in. "They found her," Teo-

filo yelled. "She's okay."

Papa said, "When it got dark the girl saw lights from a car on the highway and made her way back there. Someone picked her up and took her home. It's stopped snowing."

"See," Mama said, turning to me. "I told you she'd be all right."

I crept off to bed, but at first I couldn't go to sleep. When I did, I had a fearsome nightmare and woke up screaming and scared Mama.

Morning came, clear and cold. Mama fixed breakfast, but I wasn't hungry. As soon as I'd dressed I went outside and looked to see the first of the sunlight on the Arrow's high peak. Snow was heavy up there but here it had started to melt on the ground and to slide off the trees. Icicles began to break off the eaves of the house.

The boys decided to slide downhill before the snow was gone. Teofilo got out the old car fender we use as a sled and Jerry and he went trudging up a slope. They didn't even ask me to slide with them. I didn't deserve to play with them, I thought, even if they didn't know what I'd done. I was a criminal.

Mama kept calling me to come in to breakfast. To please her, I ate part of a tortilla and drank some coffee. Then I said, "I guess I'll take some tortillas to eat on the way and go see how Aunt Ophie made out in the storm."

Mama thought that was a good idea and I bundled

up and hurried away. I climbed up to the ledge to leave tortillas for my coyote. It might have comforted me to see him but I couldn't find even a track in the melting snow. It was too cold to wait and see if he would come and I started back to the road.

I didn't want to go to Aunt Ophie's. She would say something about the statue and I didn't want to talk about that.

I didn't want to go home, either.

Suddenly I thought, I'll go to the Mission, it will be quiet in the church. I'll sit and look at the colored windows with the pictures of saints and things, red and purple and gold . . .

When we go there in the car we go down our road and along the highway, but from here I could take a shortcut between two hills and be there in a little while.

Thank goodness no one else was there inside the church. I looked at the sanctuary lamp burning red and at a candle someone had lit before the statue of the Blessed Mother.

Suddenly I knelt before her and began to tell her the awful thing I'd done to Lucy. Then I told her all about Saint Francis and the coyote so that she would understand why I had been so angry and so hurt. I told her how much it had meant to me to make that beautiful thing and how I still wished I could do it, but how everything about it seemed to be forever spoiled. I begged her to take good care

of the coyote, wherever he was, for I loved him very much. I explained that it was my fault, not his, that everything had gone wrong.

I don't often feel like praying, but this time I had so very much to say. It helps to tell someone all about everything. It helped just to be kneeling there.

I heard a sound and when I got off my knees I saw that Father Antonio had come in. He was sitting in a back pew reading a book.

The next thing I knew, I was telling him everything I had told the Blessed Mother.

"That's very bad, Francie." Father Antonio spoke in a sad, tired voice.

It came to me that he must be awfully tired of hearing about people's sins. "What'll I do, Father?"

"You know what might have happened?"

"Yes, Father, I did it on purpose. I really wanted to hurt that girl."

"And now you feel bad. You feel sorry."

"Oh, yes."

"And you think because you feel bad, it makes it all right?"

"Oh, no, it's worse than that. Lots."

"It's hard to believe it of you, Francie." Father Antonio sighed. "I mean, that you would want to hurt someone. But you did want to, didn't you?"

"Yes, and you know I wouldn't hurt a puppy or a kitten or anything . . ." I didn't know what more to say.

"Remember that day we were talking, you and I? When you were asking about Saint Francis? Yes, and we were saying how he had been such a rich and such a proud young man. And then he learned that he had been proud about the wrong things. And after he learned that, everything was different. You remember, don't you?"

"I was too sure, wasn't I, Father? Too proud?"

"You think so?"

I nodded.

I knew what he was going to say next, so I said it first. "I have to go to Lucy, don't I, Father? I have to tell her how I really wanted to hurt her and how sorry I am now. I have to ask for pardon for what I did to her, don't I?"

"That'll be hard. You won't like it, but that must be your first step."

"I'll go right now, before I back down."

Then I thought of something else that was troubling me. "Father Antonio, I really don't think it was very nice of Miss Pierce to do what she did. She must have known how I felt—how *could* she say that Lucy ought to help me with my very own statue? When I first showed it to her she made me think she liked it a lot. All morning long I was so pleased, then it was as if she'd hit me when she said that I needed Lucy to help with it. Father, *how could she?*" I felt ready to cry again.

"Well, I don't know." Father Antonio shook his

head. "She didn't mean to hurt, Francie. At first, I guess she was all excited over your wonderful idea, and then, later, she thinks of improvements in the work. Maybe if she'd thought about it more, maybe by the next day even, she would have put it to you so you'd know she was trying to help you make a better thing than maybe you could by yourself. What do you think?"

I didn't know what to think.

He added, "Anyway, you talk about that to her. Probably she liked the statue so much she wanted to have it perfect. Maybe she'll explain she didn't mean to hurt your pride."

Pride was getting to be an awful word. "Well, I'll have to tell her I'm sorry I got mad . . . I better go to Lucy."

I didn't cut back through the hills. From here it was nearer to go along the highway. I walked fast, in a hurry to get it over with. Once I'd talked to Lucy, everything would be all right again.

As I walked along I began to feel more cheerful and I heard a meadowlark. I love the way they drop their songs down as they fly. This one knew that it was spring, even with melting snow on the ground.

I hoped to find Lucy outdoors, but I didn't see her. I began to worry. What if she'd caught a bad cold and already had pneumonia. Feeling weak and frightened, I went up on her front porch.

Lucy's mother must have looked out the window

and seen me coming for she opened the door before I found the courage to knock. I stared at her and gulped, wondering if she knew what I'd done.

But it was all right. "Do you want to see Lucy?" she asked, smiling at me. "You'll have to come in. I won't let her go outdoors today, she got too chilled yesterday."

"Is she all right?"

"Fine. Come in."

I began to feel better. Perhaps, after all, even Lucy didn't know that I'd deliberately gotten her lost. For just a second, I felt tempted not to say anything about it. But I knew I had to.

"She's in her room. This way."

Lucy, in a blue bathrobe, lay on top of her bed, reading.

She looked up. "Oh," she said, and I couldn't tell whether she sounded friendly or not.

I talked fast. "I'm sorry I got so mad. You know, about the statue. And there's something else . . ."

She said, "Miss Pierce sure didn't like it when we began to shout at each other. I guess that's why I didn't find that shortcut. I was too mad to think."

"Oh, Lucy. There *wasn't* any shortcut! I was so furious at you I told you the wrong way. On purpose."

Lucy sat straight up. "On purpose? You tried to kill me! What kind of a friend are you? Is that the way Indians really are?"

I didn't wait for more. I turned and banged out of the house and began to run. I wanted to get back to my mountain and die.

Fifteen

THE NEXT day, after we'd been to church and had our Sunday dinner, I started out to take food to the coyote. It seemed to me that, since all else had failed, the only good thing left for me to do was to keep on trying to feed him.

I didn't know how I was going to face Miss Pierce on Monday. And how in the world could I sit in the same classroom with Lucy?

A warm sun beat down to melt the snow that was left, wild lilacs made the air smell like a perfume store, and birds sang spring songs. Little frogs were sounding lively down by the creek. They were singing about warm water and polliwogs. All this should have made me feel better, but it didn't.

Then I heard pounding hoofs and I looked up to see Lucy riding toward me as fast as Redbird would go.

"Oh, Francie!" she yelled, "I need help. Something terrible has happened!"

"Get my brothers then."

"I don't know where they are. Francie, it's awful. There's a coyote in a trap. He's half-dead and I don't know how to get him out!"

"Oh," I said, my heart turning over. "A very big coyote? Where is he? I didn't know there was a trapper around."

"Not very big. He's not on the Reservation. I found him near the fence up on that other hill, in the pasture the dairy uses for heifers. Oh, hurry! We must get him out."

I told myself, it *can't* be my coyote. It's too far away. But just the same I was frightened. "Will Redbird ride double? Let me jump on."

Before I had time to get on Redbird, we saw the best sight that ever could be. Teofilo and Jerry came jogging up the road on the burros. We both started shouting at them, trying to tell them what the trouble was, but we talked so fast they couldn't understand. I hurried to jump on the third burro. I didn't have a rope to put on him but I knew he'd follow the others.

"Lead off," I yelled at Lucy. "We'll follow."

"What's wrong?" my brothers kept demanding.

110

"Lucy found a coyote in a trap. We've got to help him."

"For gosh sakes," said Teofilo, "is that all?"

"Hurry," I begged, kicking the burro with my heels. "Hurry after Lucy, she'll show us."

Lucy went shooting up the road past Aunt Ophie's and we urged the burros into a lope. Redbird and Lucy cut off to the right through a narrow draw that took us a mile or two to the south fence of the Reservation.

The poor old burros had never gone so fast in all their lives, but even so, the way seemed terribly long. We didn't slow down once. We galloped right across a stream and kept on going. I prayed, "Don't let it be my coyote, but help us to help whatever coyote it is." It couldn't be mine, I thought. The hills were full of coyotes.

Lucy turned and started up the hill along a fence line, and then we couldn't hurry. The hill was too steep and Redbird and the burros were puffing too hard. I jumped off and started scrambling along on foot. I could go faster that way. I got ahead of everyone and kept on going. Lucy cried, "Keep watching across the fence. He's along there, a little further up."

I was the first to reach him. I squirmed through the barbed wire—and stared in horror at my poor little coyote. His eyes were open but he didn't seem to be seeing. He was breathing as if every breath

hurt and his swollen tongue hung out of his mouth.

He was caught in two traps. One held a front paw, one a back, and he lay in a twisted, tormented position. He was all hide and bones, the saddest animal I'd ever seen. I was trying to catch my breath, and at the same time I was crying and fumbling at the traps.

The boys and Lucy fastened their animals to fence posts and came scrambling through the wire.

Later, I had time to think that I'd never seen my brothers' attitudes change so fast.

"Oh, the poor little devil," Teofilo said, and Jerry started crying. Lucy was crying as hard as I was.

"Let's see now," said Teofilo. "I know how these things work. Jerry, you go get a rope off the burro. We got to tie his mouth shut so he won't bite when we get him out."

I gulped back tears. "He won't bite, he's too sick."

"He'll die pretty soon anyway," Teofilo said. "Let's see—you press here. Gee, it works hard. I think he's been in here a long time. Jerry, you help."

Finally, they got the little coyote free and put him down on the grass. There were deep, bloody grooves in his paws. He sighed, a long quivering sigh, and I thought he was dying. Then the loud, rasping breathing started again.

"Got pneumonia, I bet," Teofilo said. "What'll we do with him now?"

Lucy said, "We have to get him to a safe place. But we better get some water into him quick. He's

112

partly dying of thirst."

"Let's take him to the stream back there," Teofilo suggested.

I pulled him gently under the bottom wire of the fence and picked him up. He didn't weigh much. I hurried along on foot and the others caught up with me. I dipped the coyote's mouth into the water and his tongue moved, but he didn't lap or swallow. I laid him down and dribbled water from my hand into his mouth, carefully. Too much and he might choke, for he seemed unconscious. Lucy began rubbing his injured paws to get the circulation back. They were as cold as if he were dead.

Then he swallowed and that was hopeful. I kept dribbling in more water and he continued swallowing. He moved his head back and forth weakly. His eyes were glazed and mattery, but finally he shut them as if he were feeling more comfortable.

The blood must have started back into the paws Lucy was rubbing, for he twitched his legs. I began on his other paws; they were cold too. Jerry stroked his thin belly and Teofilo rubbed his back gently.

"What can we do for him?" Lucy asked. "We've got to do something."

"How do you cure pneumonia?" Jerry wanted to know.

Lucy looked puzzled. "I don't know. Good nursing, I guess. Maybe we ought to get him some water from that magic spring you showed me that day."

I picked him up. "I know where we can take him."
I said to the boys, "Remember that old deserted
cabin up on the mountain where we used to play?
No one ever uses it now. We'll shut him in there."

"Why can't we take him home?"

I thought about that. "It wouldn't do," I decided.
"You know how grownups are. They'd say he's a
wild animal and he'd bite us, he might have some
awful disease or something. We better not tell anyone about him. Someone would be sure to want to
kill him."

I started walking again. The others rode along
beside us. It was only about a mile to the cabin and
there we found some old gunnysacks and made a
bed for him. "What food should we make him
swallow?" Lucy asked. "Milk? Soup?"

"Either would be good." I turned to Jerry. "Look,
here's an old pan. See if it leaks. If it doesn't, take it
to the magic spring and get some water. It might
help him."

"Here's a bottle I found. That's better. Carry it in
this," Teofilo offered.

Lucy said, "I'm going back to the dairy. I know
where they keep their medicines for the cows and
I'll sneak out a syringe and some antibiotic. Why
can't we give him a shot? They give cows shots for
everything."

"Sure." Teofilo looked pleased. "I know how. I've
helped Papa with cows and horses. You put it in the

114

muscle."

"I'll go right now," Lucy volunteered. "And I'll get a can of soup, too, out of the cupboard."

"Don't forget a can opener then. Oh, Lucy, you do have good ideas!" I couldn't believe she was the person I'd been so angry at. I didn't have much time to think about it then, but I knew that Lucy had forgiven me too.

Lucy left and Jerry took the bottle and headed for the magic spring. Teofilo and I stroked the coyote.

After a time, Teofilo said, "He sure has a lot of fleas. But they aren't leaving him so he can't be dying yet."

"Look at all those ticks." We started killing fleas and ticks. "Poor thing! He couldn't scratch all that time in the traps."

"I hate traps. I never knew before how bad they are."

I had a dreadful thought. "Teofilo, there must be more traps! Oh, what will we do?"

Teofilo started for the door. "I'm going to look."

I crouched beside my coyote and prayed as hard as ever I could.

Sixteen

JERRY WAS the first one back. I poured a little of the magic-spring water into the pan I'd found and kept moistening the coyote's lips.

Much later, Teofilo came. "There is a trapper, all right. Got a trap-line. I saw him."

"Who?"

"I don't know. Some white guy. I hid and watched. I didn't see him right away. I'd smoothed the dirt over where we got the coyote out, and I'd thrown the traps and the stake in the brush. It was good I happened to do that first. I heard him coming and I hid. Better that he shouldn't know any kids got a coyote loose. He looked around where the coyote had been, but I'd thrown a lot of leaves around

and maybe he couldn't remember just where he'd set those traps. I don't know. Anyway, he went on and I kept hiding and following."

I hated to ask, but I did. "Were there others in traps?"

Teofilo nodded, but all he'd say was, "Oh, a few."

Jerry is awful about gruesome matters. "What did he do, beat 'em over the head?"

Teofilo told him to shut up. "Anyway," he went on, "then I knew where he set each trap. You couldn't tell if you didn't see him do it. You could look around and never see a trap. They're all covered over. Now I'm waiting for him to be good and gone, then Jerry and I'll go over there. We'll spring all the traps. We'll poke them with sticks, then we'll take the sticks out so's he won't think anyone's sprung them. We'll leave them sprung and he won't know."

"We've got to cover up all our tracks real good."

Teofilo nodded.

"But then he'll only set them again," I said.

"I bet he doesn't come very often. Look how long he left the coyote."

"Maybe he didn't like getting out in the cold weather. We'll have to see. I figure he checks about every three days. Maybe every two days, but I bet not."

"How awful!" I said. "Do you think that if he finds he never catches anything he'll go away?"

"Well, I should think so."

"What if he comes on the Reservation?"

"Maybe Papa won't let him."

"Ho," I said. "Everyone thinks there's too many coyotes. The Indians wouldn't care if he trapped."

"Papa could say that their dogs would get caught. I've heard of little calves getting in traps—and couldn't deer?"

I started to cry again. "And if the coyote gets well, we can't let him go or he'll get in another trap. What'll we do?"

"Aw," said Teofilo, "he'll probably die anyway."

I was still crying when Lucy came back. From the way I looked she thought that the coyote had died. Teofilo reassured her. "He's still breathing."

"Well then, let's don't cry yet. Look what I got. And even directions for how much to give different animals."

We began reading them. "Look," Lucy pointed out, "it says 'dogs, cats, minks, rabbits, foxes.' *Foxes.* That's good enough. But who would be giving shots to foxes? Do people raise tame foxes? Or minks?"

We didn't know. "But look here," I said excitedly. "It says that most sick animals properly treated with antibiotics should get better within forty-eight hours. That's good."

Teofilo was reading further. "It says to inject deep within the fleshy muscles of hip, rump, round or thigh. What's round? Anyway, he hasn't any fleshy anything, he's all skinny. But I can find a muscle I

118

bet. How much does it say to give him?"

"For one that weighs fifteen to twenty pounds it would be from three-fourths to one cc. He'd weigh that much, wouldn't he?"

"Sure, I'll give him one cc." And in the most professional manner Teofilo began measuring into the syringe. Lucy looked at him admiringly and even I was impressed.

"Papa always puts on a dab of alcohol before he gives a shot, but I don't think it matters." Teofilo kept feeling the coyote until he thought he'd found a proper muscle, then he jabbed in the needle neatly and pushed in the thick white medicine. The coyote jerked feebly.

"Here." Teofilo handed Lucy the syringe. "You'll have to wash it—wash it real good in plain water. This thick stuff makes the syringe stick if you don't get it all cleaned out. Don't lose the needle. I've got to give him shots twice a day."

"I guess we can't really sterilize it, but good washing ought to do. Oh, I brought a can of soup, too. And some salve for his hurt paws. We ought to clean those sores and wash out his eyes."

I opened the can and diluted a little of the soup with water. I didn't dilute it very much and when I got enough in his mouth the coyote swallowed. I began to feel more hopeful.

"We better go fix those other traps," Teofilo said to Jerry. "Come on."

"Other traps? Oh!" Lucy's voice sounded faint.

As the boys left, I told her what Teofilo had discovered and what he planned to do about it.

"That hill pasture belongs to the dairy. Somebody there must have told the man he could trap in the pasture. Probably the dairymen think there are too many coyotes. Francie, this is just terrible. The traps will catch raccoons and possums and foxes and bobcats and everything! And this is spring—the animals have their babies to look after."

"Can't your father stop the trapper?"

"I don't think so. He's the head milker, but he wouldn't have any say about anything like this. Oh, *why* are people so mean?"

I couldn't answer. I didn't know.

We got a little more of the soup into our coyote and he swallowed some more water from the magic spring. Then he seemed to go to sleep in a natural and comfortable way. Lucy said that a good sleep was like medicine. "He probably never really rested, just sort of half-slept like people do when they are delirious. Not a deep sleep."

"Lucy," I said after a while. "I'll tell you something that will let you know why we just have to save this coyote. You saw him one time when he was well and happy. The boys yelled at him and he ran off."

"Oh? Was it this one? I remember. And I was mad at your brothers for scaring him."

"So was I. But look at those boys now. They feel

120

as bad as we do."

Lucy nodded. "They never really saw before how mean people are to coyotes."

"Well, anyway," I went on, then almost stopped because this was a touchy subject. "Anyway, you know that statue I made. This is that very coyote. I saw him right after I got the idea of having Saint Francis hold a coyote. When I first saw him he seemed to be a sign that it was right to put a coyote in Saint Francis's arms. Lucy, I thought I was making a wonderful thing . . ."

I couldn't say any more. I just looked at her, feeling helpless.

Lucy said, "You can still fix that statue, Francie."

I shook my head. "Not now. It's gone. I threw it away. I didn't want to see it again."

"Oh, Francie, you didn't!"

"Yes, I did."

"Well then, you can start all over. Probably it will come out exactly right, now. And Francie, you *do* know more than I do about coyotes and things like that. Indians must know more about earth and animals than other people do. Indians are nearer to real things."

I hesitated. "Well, maybe." It was all I could think of to say.

Lucy didn't seem to know what to say, either. But it didn't matter. We each knew what the other was feeling.

Pretty soon Lucy said, "I can't bear it if he dies." She crouched beside the coyote. "We ought to keep turning him a lot. After being trapped so long he needs to move."

"He needs lots of care. And we have to go to school."

We were still pondering this problem when the boys came back.

Teofilo thought he had the answer. "We'll just ditch school."

"But we can't. They'll catch us."

"We could pretend to be sick."

"Then Mama would keep us in the house."

For once, one of my brothers had a good idea, though at first I wasn't sure. Jerry said, "Why don't we take him to Aunt Ophie's? You and her seem to get along."

I was doubtful, for you never can be sure how Aunt Ophie is going to react to anything. But then I thought, what else can we do?

Lucy said, "We better hurry up and take him, if we're going to. It's getting late. Tomorrow we can go to see him first thing after school. I can talk my mother into letting me go straight to your house from school. It would be quicker that way."

"All right," I said. "All we can do is try."

Seventeen

"I can carry him in front of me on the burro," Teofilo said.

"No. I'm going to walk and carry him. He'll be more comfortable that way." I picked up the coyote and started down the trail for Aunt Ophie's.

As I hurried along I looked up at the mountain. Up there somewhere the coyote had been born—and how I wished he would live to return to his own place! There were shadows on the slopes now, though the snowy peak was still bright with sun. This one warm day had melted all the lower snows.

None of us talked much along the way. We were too worried. Everything depended on Aunt Ophie.

When we reached her place I went into the house

124

while the others tied their animals.

Aunt Ophie was surprised, all right.

"What you got there? A danged coyote?"

"He's been in traps for a long time. Aunt Ophie, look."

One thing about Aunt Ophie is that when she gets mad she's about the maddest person I've ever seen. Now she wasn't mad at the coyote, she was mad at the trapper.

She was going strong by the time the others came in the house. "I hate trappers worse than anything! Best dog I ever had got in a trap and the trapper killed him. I'll pull up every one of those traps and throw them away. I'll bust that trapper one in the nose. I'll run him clean out of the country . . ."

Jerry said, "You bet. Run him out."

"These traps were over in that hill pasture where the dairy heifers graze," Lucy told her.

"He's got no business being that close to the Reservation. He'll catch every dog on it. You just wait until I meet up with him!"

I interrupted to ask, "Can you make the coyote well?"

"Let's have a good look. Oh, the poor thing. If a person wants to kill something they should shoot it dead, not leave it to get like this." Aunt Ophie peered into the coyote's eyes, put down her head and listened to his breathing.

"Francie, can you find a big piece of cardboard?

Look in the back room. I think I got a box like dresses come in from the store."

Wondering, I went to look.

I heard Aunt Ophie telling the boys, "You two go down in the creek bed and dig me up a lot of yerba mansa roots. And you, little girl, will you go pick a lot of black sage and get some of that stuff white people call artemesia? Do you know what it is? Sometimes it's called romerilla."

"Yes, ma'am." Lucy hurried off.

I rummaged around, thinking that Aunt Ophie never threw anything away and maybe it was a good thing. Finally, I found the box she wanted.

"Good," she said. "Now get me my big scissors. And after that, look in the cupboards. Somewhere I've got a jug of water from the magic spring. I always keep some fresh on hand."

I found the water and Aunt Ophie said, "Now put it to boil in two pots. Put some more wood in the stove."

As I was doing this, Aunt Ophie cut the cardboard and shaped it into a funnel. "Now find me some string and we'll fasten it so's it'll stay this shape."

The boys came back with the yerba mansa and Aunt Ophie went to work with a knife, cutting off the tops of the plants, splitting the red roots.

When Lucy came in Aunt Ophie ordered her to put the sage leaves and the artemesia into one of the pots on the stove. She dropped the roots into

another pot, then sat down to look at the coyote.

"This animal needs steaming to make him breathe better. He needs lots of care."

"Aunt Ophie, will he get well?"

"He's very sick, Francie. But I've saved lots of animals and lots of people, too. Now you help me and I'll show you how to make him breathe this good steam from the weeds."

"What's the yerba mansa for?" Jerry wanted to know.

"That's for the tea I'll give him to make him swallow. Yerba mansa tea made from water from the magic spring will cure anything, even a horse with lockjaw. Now put some of the boiling weed water into a smaller pot and we'll start him breathing better. See, he'll get the steam through this funnel."

"Mama doesn't know about the coyote," I told Aunt Ophie.

"We won't tell her. People would think I was crazy, nursing a coyote. Now you help me. Hold up his head and he'll have to breathe this."

I never felt so grateful to anyone. My Aunt Ophie is wonderful.

Eighteen

In the night I heard coyotes on the mountain. I wondered if my poor little one would ever sing with those others. I wondered if he were listening to them, and what he thought.

How does a trapped coyote feel when he hears the free ones on the hills?

It was torture to go to school in the morning. I didn't know whether my coyote was dead or alive. I sat beside Lucy on the bus. We didn't talk much except that Lucy said, "At least we know your Aunt Ophie will do everything she can. That's some comfort."

Compared to my worry about the coyote, my other problem, Miss Pierce, seemed small. I found I

wasn't in the least mad at her now, but I couldn't bear the thought of having a talk with her. I was too sad about the statue to want to discuss it just now. Some time I knew I'd explain how sorry I was I'd behaved so badly, but this was not the day for explanations.

Miss Pierce must have noticed that things had changed, for when Lucy and I went into the room together she smiled at us. We both smiled back, though this day it wasn't easy to smile about anything.

All day I thought about the coyote and I knew he was all Lucy was thinking about too.

At recess and at lunchtime we hurried out of class together. I could see that Lucy didn't want to talk with Miss Pierce any more than I did. I grew more and more nervous as the day wore on, sure that, just before closing time, she would ask us to stay a minute. But she didn't.

As soon as the bell rang we headed for the bus. We were the first ones on, Teofilo and Jerry were the next. That afternoon the bus seemed to go slower than it ever had. Lucy came with us when we met Mama at the foot of the road.

I told her that Lucy and the boys and I were going to see Aunt Ophie. "And after that, I'd like to walk part way home with Lucy," I added.

"Okay," Mama agreed. "Isn't it good that the days are getting longer now?"

She must have been surprised that we didn't want any peanut-butter sandwiches after we got home. All of us were in a hurry to start for Aunt Ophie's.

When we were nearly there Teofilo remembered something. "I went and forgot. I left the syringe and the shot medicine in the cabin yesterday. Me and Jerry can go get it."

"All right," I said, "but be quick about it."

"Maybe your Aunt Ophie has him better by now," Lucy said hopefully as we neared her place.

Aunt Ophie opened the door for us. "He's still alive. Maybe the best thing would be for you to carry him out and put him down in the sun for a while. Sunshine is good medicine. One thing for sure—he's not going to jump up and run away."

The coyote looked a little better because Aunt Ophie had cleaned out his eyes and doctored his wounded paws. But he still breathed as if it were hard work.

We found a nice place for him where the grass was warm with sun. He seemed to like it for he found strength to lift his head. Perhaps he smelled the air from the mountain. I wondered if he remembered hunting mice in the high meadows, if he thought of how good the morning dew would feel on his scarred paws. It was his mountain, where he belonged.

He sighed, dropped his head and went to sleep.

I said, "Maybe he dreams about his mountain."

Lucy's voice sounded strange. "I think he's already there."

I looked again and then I knew what Lucy meant. Our coyote was dead and Lucy was crying.

After a while Lucy said, "Francie, you just have to make that statue. Saint Francis and the coyote. It is something very important now."

All I said was, "Lucy, please. Will you help me?"

We couldn't talk any more. The boys came and they felt almost as awful as we did. Aunt Ophie handed them a shovel and that cheered them a little. My brothers always have to have something to do.

Lucy asked, "Can't we take him up on his mountain and bury him there?"

And that's what we did, under a big oak where roots could find him and perhaps turn him into leaves to live in the wind.

Lucy and I shared our sorrow with each other. It was some days before we could bring ourselves to start work on the statue because we'd start crying instead.

But Lucy was the strong one. She said, "We can't keep on like this, Francie. We have something too important to do. It is absolutely the only thing we can do now for the coyote."

I knew what she meant. Unless we made Saint Francis and the coyote, the coyote would have lived and died for nothing.

So we went to work, slowly and carefully this

time. And Aunt Ophie helped us. I had been afraid that she wouldn't because of Lucy being a white girl, but she was as nice to Lucy as she was to me. Maybe she was learning about things, just as I was.

If you ever come to a mountain called Higher Than The Arrow, look for an Indian Mission church at its base. Go inside and you'll find a little statue. Perhaps it is not the most beautiful one in the world but it is the only one like it. The hands of Saint Francis are scarred by the stigmata and the paws of the coyote are scarred by traps.

As a young girl growing up in San Diego, Judy Van der Veer's ambition was to live on a ranch full of animals and to write stories about them. Her early dreams have been more than fulfilled for today she lives on a 600-acre ranch in the hill country of Southern California, near the town of Ramona, where she raises horses and cows and a variety of other animals, and where she writes about these creatures with great love and understanding. She is the author of a number of distinguished adult books (*The River Pasture, Brown Hills, November Grass, A Few Happy Ones, My Valley In The Sky*) and is a regular contributor to the *Christian Science Monitor*. With the publication of *Hold The Rein Free* in 1966 Miss Van der Veer won immediate recognition as an outstanding author of junior novels.